BEOWULF

THE STORY OF BEOWULF

Translated from the Anglo Saxon
into Modern English Prose by
ERNEST J. B. KIRTLAN

CLYDESDALE

First published in 1853 by D.C. HEATH & CO., PUBLISHERS

First Clydesdale Press Edition 2016

Clydesdale Press books may be purchased in bulk at special discounts for sales promotion, corporate gifts, fund-raising, or educational purposes. Special editions can also be created to specifications. For details, contact the Special Sales Department, Skyhorse Publishing, 307 West 36th Street, 11th Floor, New York, NY 10018 or info@skyhorsepublishing.com.

Clydesdale Press™ is a pending trademark of Skyhorse Publishing, Inc.®, a Delaware corporation.

Visit our website at www.skyhorsepublishing.com.

10 9 8 7 6 5 4 3 2 1

Library of Congress Cataloging-in-Publication Data is available on file.

Series design by Brian Peterson
Cover illustration credit: iStock

Print ISBN: 978-1-945186-07-3
Ebook ISBN: 978-1-945186-15-8

Printed in the United States of America

CONTENTS

Note as to Use of Appendix

I have relegated to the Appendix all notes of any considerable length. The reader is advised to consult the Appendices wherever directed in the end notes. He will then have a much clearer conception of the principal characters and events of the poem.

Introduction

'Beowulf' may rightly be pronounced the great national epic of the Anglo-Saxon race. Not that it exalts the race so much as that it presents the spirit of the Anglo-Saxon peoples, the ideals and aims, the manners and customs, of our ancestors, and that it does so in setting before us a great national hero. Beowulf himself was not an Anglo-Saxon. He was a Geat-Dane; but he belonged to that confraternity of nations that composed the Teutonic people. He lived in a heroic age, when the songs of the wandering singers were of the great deeds of outstanding men. The absolute epic of the English people has yet to be written. To some extent Arthur, though a British King—that is to say, though he was King of the Celtic British people, who were subsequently driven into the West, into Cornwall and Wales and Strathclyde, by our Saxon ancestors—became nationalized by our Anglo-Norman ancestors as a typical King of the English people. He has become the epic King of the English in the poetry of Tennyson. It is always a mystery to the writer that no competent singer among us has ever laid hands upon our own Saxon hero, King Alfred. It is sometimes said that there is nothing new under the sun, that there is nothing left for the modern singer to sing about, and that the realm of possible musical production is fast vanishing out of view. Certainly this is not true of poetry. Both Alfred and Arthur are waiting for the sympathetic voice that will tell forth to the world the immortal splendour of their personalities. And just as the Anglo-Normans idealized Arthur as a hero-king of the English nation, though he really fought against the English, so the Saxon singer of Beowulf has idealized this Geatish chieftain, and in some way set him forth as the idealized chieftain of the Teutonic race.

Beowulf is an Anglo-Saxon poem which consists of 3182 lines. It is written in the alliterative verse of our ancestors in the Anglo-Saxon tongue, which, though the mother-tongue of the English, is yet more difficult to read for the Englishman than Latin or Greek. One wonders whether any genuine Anglo-Saxon epic existed, and has been destroyed in the passing of the centuries. The curious feature about this poem is that it concerns a man who was not an Anglo-Saxon. Our poem is written in the West-Saxon dialect. The original poem was probably in Northumbrian, and was translated into West Saxon during the period of literary efflorescence in the West Saxon Court. We do not know whether it was a translation or whether it was original, though the latter is, I believe, the prevailing opinion. Arnold has put forth what may be called the missionary theory of its origin. He believes that both the choice of subject and the grade of culture may be connected with the missionary efforts of the English Church of those days to extend Christianity in Friesland and further east. 'It does not seem improbable that it was in the interest of the spread of Christianity that the composer of *Beowulf*—perhaps a missioner, perhaps a layman attached to the mission—was attracted to the Scandinavian lands; that he resided there long enough to become thoroughly steeped in the folk-lore and local traditions; that he found the grand figure of Beowulf the Geat predominant in them; and that, weaving into an organic whole those which he found suitable to his own purpose, he composed an epic which, on his return home, must soon have become known to all the lovers of English song.'[1] Dr. Sarrazin thought this unknown poet might have been the famous Cynewulf. Arnold, chiefly on stylistic grounds, differs from this opinion. This is Arnold's opinion: 'Sagas, either in the Danish dialect or that of the Geats—more probably the latter—were current in the Scandinavian countries in the seventh century. Among these sagas, that of Beowulf the Geat must have had a prominent place; others celebrated Hygelac his uncle, Hnaef the Viking, the wars of the Danes and the Heathobards, of the Danes and the Swedes. About the end of the century missionaries from England are known to have been busy in Friesland and Denmark, endeavouring to convert the natives to Christianity. Some one of these, whose mind had a turn for literature and dwelt with joy upon the traditions of the past, collected or learnt by heart a number of these sagas, and, taking that of *Beowulf* as a basis, and weaving some others into his work, composed an epic poem to which, although it contains the record of those adventures, the heroic scale of the figure who accomplishes them all imparts a real unifying epic interest.' Whatever may be the truth as to its origin, there it lies in the British Museum in its unique MS. as a testimony to all ages of the genius of the Anglo-Saxon race.

Now it will be quite naturally asked: What do we learn from *Beowulf* of the genius and spirit of that race from which we are sprung?

The one outstanding fact, as it appears to the writer, is the co-operative principle. And this principle stands in almost violent opposition to the ruling principle of the modern world, in which society is divided into a number of mutually opposite sections or classes, whose interests clash with fatal results to individual and corporate well-being. In this poem we see the whole community, from the King to the churl, bound by one common interest. King and chieftain and thane and churl freely intermingle and converse. They eat and drink and sleep under one common roof, or at least in one common enclosure. *Tempora mutantur!* but the idea of social interaction and mutual interdependence never found more vivid or real expression than in the pictures presented in *Beowulf* of Hart, the Great Hall of Hrothgar, and in the Court and township of Hygelac, King of the Geats. In the Hall of Hart, Hrothgar and his Queen and his courtiers sit at the high table on the dais, and the lower orders at the long table down the hall. The spears and shields adorn the walls. After the evening meal, the singer, or scop, as he is called, to the accompaniment of the harp, tells forth the deeds of some ancient feud, such as that of Finn and the Danes or the Fight at Finnsburgh, or the feud of the Danes and the Heathobards, in which Freawaru, Hrothgar's daughter, and Ingeld figure so tragically. Then the benches are removed, and the rude beds are spread out on the floor of the Great Hall and they seek 'evening rest.' The whole is a picture of fraternal and paternal government. If Grendel, the Fen-monster, carries away one of their number, then there is weeping and lamentation. The King and the Queen and the nobility and the commonalty are all concerned in the tragedy. The loss of one is the loss of all. When Aeschere is slain by Grendel's mother, Hrothgar thus bewails his loss: 'Seek no more after joy; sorrow is renewed for the Danish folk. Aeschere is dead, he who was my wise counsellor and my adviser and my comrade in arms, when in time of war we defended ourselves; . . . but now the hand lieth low which bestowed every kind of joy upon you.' And in the end of the poem it is said of Beowulf that he was 'most gentle to his folk.' The King was king only 'for his folk.' The interest of his folk, their physical and moral well-being, was his chief solicitude.

But not only was this so within any one nation or tribe, but there was a sense of comradeship and mutual responsibility among those of various tribes and nations. When Beowulf the Geat hears in Gautland of the raids of Grendel upon Hart, he commands his folk to make ready a boat that he may fare across the sea to the help of Hrothgar, because 'he was lacking in warriors.' Beowulf's whole mission in Hart was the discharge of a solemn obligation of help from the strong to the weak. He announces to Hrothgar that he is come 'to cleanse Hart of ill,' and this he feels he *must* do. 'Woe is me if I preach not the gospel!' cried St. Paul. 'Woe is me if I help not the weak and cleanse not the demon-infested palace of my kinsman!' cried Beowulf. 'Weird goes as he willeth'; that is, Fate must be submitted to. And Fate hath willed that he should help the weak and 'cleanse the ill.'

Then there is the tremendous sense of loyalty on the part of the folk to their king or chieftain. The idea of the 'Comitatus' bound the folk to their leaders. Nothing more disgraceful could be conceived than the desertion of the leader. Terrible were the reproaches hurled at the trembling cowards who had hurried away into the woods, to save their own skins, whilst their King Beowulf wrestled with the dragon, the enemy of the people. 'Yea, death is better for any earl than a life of reproach.' Loyalty, a passionate loyalty to the King, was the greatest of virtues, and disloyalty and cowardice the greatest of vices. Society was an organic whole, bound together by the bands of loyalty and devotion to the common good.

There is, too, the fatalistic note heard all through the poem. Beowulf feels himself hard pressed by Fate. The Anglo-Saxon called Fate by the name 'Weird,' which has survived in modern English in the sense of something strange and mysterious. Weird was the God, or Goddess of Fate. Again and again in the poem we hear the solemn, minor, dirge-like refrain, 'Weird hath willed it'; 'let Weird go as it will' (chapter 6. p. 14). There is this perpetual overshadowing and almost crushing sense of some inscrutable and irresistible power that wieldeth all things and disposeth all things, which is, I believe, a pre-eminent characteristic of the Anglo-Saxon race, and accounts for the dare-devil courage of her sons upon the battle-field or on the high seas. We find it, too, in its morally less attractive form in the recrudescent pessimism of modern literature. Thomas Hardy is the lineal descendant in literature of the author of *Beowulf* when he says: 'Thus the President of the Immortals had finished his sport with poor Tess.'[2]

And closely allied to this sense of Destiny is the sombre view of life that is characteristic of the Teutonic peoples. There is none of that passionate joy in beauty and in love that we find in the Celtic literature. Life is a serious thing in *Beowulf* and with us of the Anglo-Saxon race. The scenery of *Beowulf* is massive and threatening and mist-encircled. Angry seas are boiling and surging and breaking at the foot of lofty and precipitous cliffs. Above the edge of the cliffs stretch mysterious and gloomy moorlands, and treacherous bogs and dense forests inhabited by malignant and powerful spirits, the foes of humanity. In a land like this there is no time for love-making. Eating, drinking, sleeping, fighting there make up the business of life. It is to the Celtic inflow that we owe the addition of love in our modern literature. The composer of *Beowulf* could not have conceived the Arthur Saga or the Tristram love-legend. These things belong to a later age, when Celtic and Teutonic elements were fused in the Anglo-Norman race. But we still find in our literature the sombre hues. And, after all, it is in the forest of sorrow and pain that we discover the most beautiful flowers and the subtlest perfumes.

I desire to express my indebtedness to A. J. Wyatt and William Morris for their translations; to A. J. Wyatt for his edition of the poem in the original; to Thomas Arnold for his terse and most inform-ing work on *Beowulf*; to the authors of articles in the *Encyclopaedia Britannica* and in *Chambers's Encyclopaedia* and *The Cambridge History of English Literature*.

Ernest J. B. Kirtlan.
Brighton,
November, 1913.

BEOWULF

The Prelude

Now we have heard, by inquiry, of the glory of the kings of the people, they of the Spear-Danes, how the Athelings were doing deeds of courage.[1] Full often Scyld, the son of Scef, with troops of warriors, withheld the drinking-stools from many a tribe. This earl caused terror when at first he was found in a miserable case. Afterwards he gave help when he grew up under the welkin, and worshipfully he flourished until all his neighbours over the sea gave him obedience, and yielded him tribute. He was a good king. In after-time there was born to him a son in the Court, whom God sent thither as a saviour of the people. He saw the dire distress that they formerly suffered when for a long while they were without a prince. Then it was that the Lord of Life, the Wielder of glory, gave to him glory. Famous was Beowulf.[2] Far and wide spread his fame. Heir was he of Scyld in the land of the Danes. Thus should a young man be doing good deeds, with rich gifts to the friends of his father, so that in later days, when war shall come upon them, boon companions may stand at his side, helping their liege lord. For in all nations, by praiseworthy deeds, shall a man be thriving.

At the fated hour Scyld passed away, very vigorous in spirit, to the keeping of his Lord. Then his pleasant companions carried him down to the ocean flood, as he himself had bidden them, whilst the friend of the Scyldings was wielding words, he who as the dear Lord of the Land had ruled it a long time. And there, in the haven, stood the ship, with rings at the prow, icy, and eager for the journey, the ferry of the Atheling.

Then they laid down their dear Lord the giver of rings, the famous man, on the bosom of the ship, close to the mast, where were heaps of treasures, armour trappings that had been brought from far ways. Never heard I of a comelier ship, decked out with battle-weapons and weeds of war, with swords and byrnies. In his bosom they laid many a

treasure when he was going on a far journey, into the power of the sea.
Nor did they provide for him less of booty and of national treasures
than they had done, who at the first had sent him forth, all alone o'er
the waves, when he was but a child. Then moreover they set a golden
standard high o'er his head, and let the sea take him, and gave all to
the man of the sea. Full sad were their minds, and all sorrowing were
they. No man can say soothly, no, not any hall-ruler, nor hero under
heaven, who took in that lading.[3]

THE STORY

1

Moreover the Danish Beowulf,[1] the dear King of his people, was a long time renowned amongst the folk in the cities (his father, the Prince, had gone a-faring elsewhere from this world). Then was there born to him a son, the high Healfdene; and while he lived he was ruling the happy Danish people, and war-fierce and ancient was he. Four children were born to him: Heorogar the leader of troops, and Hrothgar, and Halga the good. And I heard say that Queen Elan (wife of Ongentheow) was his daughter, and she became the beloved comrade of the Swede. Then to Hrothgar was granted good speed in warfare and honour in fighting, so that his loyal subjects eagerly obeyed him, until the youths grew doughty, a very great band of warriors. Then it burned in his mind that he would bid men be building a palace, a greater mead-hall than the children of men ever had heard of, and that he would therein distribute to young and to old, as God gave him power, all the wealth that he had save the share of the folk and the lives of men.

Then I heard far and wide how he gave commandment to many a people throughout all the world, this work to be doing, and to deck out the folkstead. In due time it happened that soon among men, this greatest of halls was now all ready. And Hart he called it, whose word had great wielding. He broke not his promise, but gave to them rings and treasures at the banquet. The hall towered on high, and the gables were wide between the horns,[2] and awaited the surging of the loathsome flames. Not long time should pass ere hatred was awakened after the battle-slaughter, twixt father-in-law and son-in-law.[3]

Then it was that the powerful sprite who abode in darkness, scarce could brook for a while that daily he heard loud joy in the hall. There was sound of harping, and the clear song of the bard.

He who knew it was telling of the beginning of mankind, and he said that the Almighty created the world, and the bright fields surrounded by water. And, exulting, He set the sun and the moon as lamps to shine upon the earth-dwellers, and adorned the world with branches and leaves. And life He was giving to every kind of living creature. So noble men lived in joy, and were all blessed till one began to do evil, a devil from hell; and this grim spirit was called Grendel. And he was a march-stepper, who ruled on the moorlands, the fens, and the stronghold. For a while he kept guard, this unhappy creature, over the land of the race of monsters, since the Creator had proscribed him. On the race of Cain the Eternal Lord brought death as vengeance, when he slew Abel. Nor did he find joy in the feud, but God for the crime drove him far thence. Thus it was that evil things came to their birth, giants and elves and monsters of the deep, likewise those giants who for a long while were striving with God Himself. And well He requited them.

2

Then he went visiting the high house after nightfall, to see how the Ring-Danes were holding it. And he found there a band of Athelings asleep after feasting. And they knew not sorrow or the misery of men. The grim and greedy wight of destruction, all fierce and furious, was soon ready for his task, and laid hold of thirty thanes, all as they lay sleeping. And away he wended, faring homeward and exulting in the booty, to revisit his dwellings filled full of slaughter. At the dawn of day the war-craft of Grendel was seen by men. Then after his feeding they set up a weeping, great noise in the morning.

The glorious Lord, the very good Atheling, sat all unblithely, and suffered great pain, and endured sorrow for his thanes, when they saw the track of the loathly one, the cursed sprite. That struggle was too strong, loathsome and long. And after but one night (no longer time was it) he did them more murder-bale, and recked not a whit the feud and the crime. Too quick was he therein. Then he who had sought elsewhere more at large a resting-place, a bed after bower, was easily found when he was shown and told most truly, by the token so clear, the hate of the hell-thane. He went away farther and faster, he who would escape the fiend. So he ruled and strove against right, he alone against all of them, until the best of houses stood quite idle. And a great while it was—the friend of the Danes suffered distress and sorrows that were great the time of twelve winters.

Then was it made known to the children of men by a sorrowful singing that Grendel was striving this while against Hrothgar, and waged hateful enmity of crime and feud for many a year with lasting strife, and would hold no truce against any man of the main host of Danes, nor put away the life-bale, or settle feud with a fee, nor did any man need to hope for brighter bettering at the hand of the banesman. The terrible monster, a dark death-shadow, was pursuing the youth and the warriors, and he fettered and ensnared them, and ever was holding night after night the misty moorlands. And, men know not ever whither workers of hell-runes wander to and fro. Thus the foe of mankind, the terrible and lonesome traveller, often he did them even greater despite. And he took up his dwelling in the treasure-decked Hall of Hart in the dark night, nor could he come near the throne the treasure of God, nor did he know His love.[4]

And great was the evil to the friend of the Danes, and breakings of heart. Many a strong one sat in council, and much they discussed what was best for stout-hearted men to do against the fearful terror. And sometimes they went vowing at their heathen shrines and offered sacrifices, and with many words pleaded that the devil himself would give them his help against this menace to the nation. For such was their custom, the hope of the heathen. And ever of Hell they thought in their hearts; the Creator they knew not, the Judge of all deeds, nor knew they the Lord God, nor could they worship the Protector of the heavens, the Wielder of glory. Woe be to that man who shall shove down a soul through hurtful malice into the bosom of the fire, and who hopes for no help nor for any change—well shall it be with that one who after his death day shall seek the Lord and desire protection in the embrace of the Father.

3

So Beowulf, son of Healfdene, ever was brooding over this time-care, nor could the brave hero avert woe. That conflict was too strong, loathsome and long, that terrible and dire distress, the greatest of night-bales which came to the people.

Then the thane of Hygelac,[5] the good man of the Geats,[6] heard from home of the deeds of Grendel. And on the day of this life he was the strongest of main of all men in the world; noble was he and powerful. He bade a fair ship be made, and said that he would be seeking the War-King, the famous prince, over the swan path, and that he needed men. And the proud churls little blamed him for that journey, though dear he was to them. They urged on the valiant man and marked the omen. The good man of the Geats had chosen champions of those who were keenest, and sought out the ship. And one, a sea-crafty man, pointed to the land-marks. Time passed by; the ship was on the waves, the boat under the cliff, and the warriors all readily went up to the stern. And the currents were swirling, with sea and sand. And men were carrying on to the naked deck bright ornaments and splendid war-armour. Then they shove forth the ship that was well bound together; and it set forth over the waves, driven by the wind, this foamy-necked ship, likest to a bird; until about the same time on the next day, the ship with its twisted stern had gone so far that the sailing men could see the land, the shining sea-cliffs, the steep mountains, and the wide sea-nesses. Then they crossed the remaining portion of the sea.[7] The Geats went up quickly on to the shore, and anchored the ship. War-shirts and war-weeds were rattling. And they gave God thanks for their easy crossing of the waves. Then the ward of the Swedes, who kept guard over the sea-cliffs, saw them carry down the gangways the bright shields and armour, all ready. And full curious thought tortured him as to who these men were. He, the thane of Hrothgar, rode down to the beach on his charger, and powerfully brandished the spear in his hand and took counsel with them.

'Who are ye armour-bearers, protected by byrnies, who come here thus bringing the high vessel over the sea, and the ringed ship over the ocean? I am he that sits at the end of the land and keeps sea-guard, so that no one more loathsome may scathe with ship-army the land of the Danes. Never have shield-bearers begun to come here more openly, yet ye seem not to know the password of warriors, the compact of kinsmen. Nor ever have I seen a greater earl upon earth, than one of your band, a warrior in armour. And except his face belie him, he that is thus weapon-bedecked is no hall-man; but a peerless one to see. Now must I know your lineage before you go farther with your false spies in the land of the Danes. Now, O ye far-dwellers and sea-farers, hear my onefold thought—haste is best in making known whence ye are come.'

4

Then the eldest gave answer, and unlocked his treasure of words, the wise one of the troop: 'We are of the race of the Geats and hearth-comrades of Hygelac. My father was well known to the folk, a noble prince was he called Ecgtheow. And he bided many winters, ere as an old man he set out on his journeys away from the dwelling places. And well-nigh every councillor throughout all the world remembered him well. We through bold thinking have come to seek thy lord, the son of Healfdene, the protector of the people. Vouchsafe to us good guidance. We have a great business with the lord of the Danes, who is far famed. Nor of this shall aught be secret as I am hoping. Well thou knowest if 'tis true as we heard say, that among the Danes some secret evil-doer, I know not what scather, by terror doth work unheard-of hostility, humiliation, and death. I may give counsel through greatness of mind to Hrothgar as to how he, the wise and good, may overcome the fiend, if ever should cease for him the baleful business and bettering come after and his troubles wax cooler, or for ever he shall suffer time of stress and miserable throes, while the best of all houses shall remain on the high stead.'

Then the watchman, the fearless warrior, as he sat on his horse, quickly made answer: 'The shield-warrior who is wide awake, shall know how to tell the difference between words and works, if he well bethink him. I can see that this band of warriors will be very welcome to the Lord of the Danes. Go ye forth, therefore, bear weapons and armour, as I will direct you. And I will command my thanes to hold against every foe, your ship in honour, new tarred as it is, and dry on the sands, until it shall carry the dearly loved man, that ship with the twisted prow, to the land of the Geats. To each of the well-doers shall it be given to escape scot-free out of the battle rush.' Then they went forth carrying their weapons. And there the ship rested, fastened by a rope, the wide-bosomed vessel secured by its anchor. The Boar[8] held life ward, bright and battle-hard and adorned with gold, over the neck-guard of the handsome Beowulf. There was snorting of the war-like-minded, whilst men were hastening, as they marched on together till they caught sight of the splendid place decked out in gold. And it was the most famous of palaces, under the heavens, of the earth-dwellers, where the ruler was biding. Its glory shone over many lands. Then the dear one in battle showed them the bright house where were the brave ones, that they might straightway make their way towards it. Then one of the warriors turned his horse round, and spake this word: 'Time it is for me to go. May the Almighty Father hold you in favour, and keep you in safety in all your journeyings. I will go to the sea-coast to keep my watch against the fierce troops.'

5

The way was paved with many coloured stones, and by it they knew the path they should take. The coat of mail shone brightly, which was firmly hand-locked. The bright iron ring sang in the armour as they came on their way in their warlike trappings at the first to the great hall. Then the sea-weary men set down their broad shields, their shields that were wondrous hard 'gainst the wall of the great house, and bowed towards the bench. And byrnies were rattling, the war-weapons of men. And the spears were standing in a row together, the weapons of the sea-men and the spear grey above. And the troop of armed men was made glorious with weapons. Then the proud chieftain asked the warriors of their kindred: 'From whence are ye bringing such gold-plated shields, grey sarks and helmets with visors, and such a heap of spears? I am the servant and messenger of Hrothgar. Never saw I so many men prouder. I trow it was for pride and not at all for banishment, but for greatness of mind that Hrothgar ye are seeking.'

Then answered the brave man, the chief of the Geats, and spake these words, hard under helmet: 'We are the comrades at table of Hygelac. Beowulf is my name. I will say fully this my errand to the son of Healfdene the famous chieftain, unto thy lord and master, if he will grant us that we may salute him who is so good.'

Then spake Wulfgar (he was Prince of the Wendels[9]). His courage was known to all, his valour and wisdom. 'I will make known to the Prince of the Danes, the Lord of the Scyldings[10] the giver of rings the famous chieftain as thou art pleading, about thy journey, and will make known to thee quickly the answer which he the good man thinks fit to give me.' Quickly he turned then to where Hrothgar was sitting, old and very grey with his troop of earls. The brave man then went and stood before the shoulders of the Lord of the Danes. Well he knew the custom of the doughty ones. Wulfgar then spoke to his lord and friend: 'Here are come faring from a far country over the wide sea, a people of the Geats, and the eldest the warriors call Beowulf. And they are asking that they may exchange words with

thee, my lord. O gladman Hrothgar, do not refuse to be talking with
them. For worthy they seem all in their war-weeds, in the judgement
of earls. At least he is a daring Prince who hither hath led this band
of warriors.'

6

Then spake Hrothgar the protector of the Danes: 'Well I knew him when he was a child, and his old father was called Ecgtheow. And to him did Hrethel of the Geats give his only daughter, and his son is bravely come here and hath sought out a gracious friend.' Then said the sea-farers who had brought the goodly gifts of the Geats there for thanks, that he the battle-brave had in his hand-grip the main craft of thirty men. 'And the holy God hath sent him for favour to us West Danes, and of this I have hope, 'gainst the terror of Grendel. I shall offer the goodman gifts for his daring. Now make thou haste and command the band of warrior kinsmen into the presence. Bid them welcome to the people of the Danes.' Then went Wulfgar even to the hall-door, and spake these words: 'My liege lord, the Prince of the East Danes, commands me to say that he knows your lineage. And ye who are bold of purpose are welcome hither over the sea-waves. Now may ye go in your war-weeds, under your visored helmets to see Hrothgar. Let your swords stay behind here, the wood and the slaughter-shafts and the issue of words.' Then the Prince rose up, and about him was many a warrior, a glorious band of thanes. And some bided there and held the battle-garments as the brave man commanded. And they hastened together under the roof of Hrothgar as the man directed them. The stout-hearted man went forward, hard under helmet till he stood by the dais.

Then Beowulf spake (and the byrny shone on him, the coat of mail, sewn by the cunning of the smith): 'O Hrothgar, all hail! I am the kinsman and comrade of Hygelac.[11] Many marvels I have set on foot in the days of my youth. The affair of Grendel was made known to me in my native land. Sea-farers told how this best of all palaces stood idle and useless to warriors, after evening light came down under the brightness of heaven. Then my people persuaded me, the best and the proudest of all my earls, O my lord Hrothgar, that I should seek thee, for they well knew my main strength. For they themselves saw how I came forth bloodstained from the power of the fiend, when I bound the five, and destroyed the giant's kin, and slew 'mongst the waves, sea-monsters by night, and suffered such dire distress, and wreaked vengeance for the strife of the Geats (for woe they were suffering), and I destroyed the fierce one. And now all alone I shall settle the affair of Grendel the deadly monster, the cruel giant. And one boon will I be asking, O Prince of the Bright Danes, thou lord of the Scyldings, Protector of warriors and friend of the folk, that thou wilt not refuse, since so far I am come, that I and my troop of earls, this crowd of brave men, may alone cleanse out Hart. I have heard say also that the monster because of his rashness recks not of weapons. And, if Hygelac the blithe-minded will be my liege lord, I will forgo to carry to the battle a sword, or broad shield all yellow; but I will engage by my hand-grip with the enemy, and strive for life, foe with foe. And he whom Death taketh shall believe in the doom of the Lord. And I doubt not he will fearlessly consume the people of the Geats, if he may prevail in the war-hall as he has often done with the strong men of the Danes. And thou shalt not need to hide my head if Death take me, for he will seize me all bloodstained, and will bury the slaughter all bloody, and will think to taste and devour me alone and without any sorrow, and will stain the glens in the moorland. And thou needest not to sorrow longer over the food of my body. And if battle take me, send to Hygelac this best of coats of mail, the noblest of garments. It is the heirloom of Hrethel the work of Weland[12]; and let Weird go as it will.'

7

Hrothgar gave answer, the protector of the Danes: 'O my friend Beowulf, now thou hast sought us, for defence and for favour. Thy father fought in the greatest of feuds. He was banesman to Heatholaf amongst the Wylfings, when for battle-terror the King of the Geats could not hold him. Thence he sought the folk of the South Danes over the welter of waves. Then first was I ruling the Danish folk, and in my youthful days possessed the costly jewels, the treasure city of heroes. Then Heregar was dead, my elder brother not living was he, the child of Healfdene. He was a better man than I was. Then a payment of money settled the matter. I sent to the Wylfings ancient presents over the sea-ridges. And he swore to me oaths. And it is to me great sorrow in my heart to tell any man what Grendel hath done in Hart through his malice, of humiliation and sudden horror. My hall-troop has grown less, the crowd of my thanes; Weird[13] has swept them towards the terror of Grendel. But easily may the good God restrain the deeds of the foolish scather. And drunken with beer the warriors full often boasted o'er the ale-cup that they would bide in the beer-hall the battle of Grendel with the terror of swords. Then was the mead-hall all bloodstained in the morning when dawn came shining, and all the benches were wet with gore, the hall with sword-blood. And so much the less did I rule o'er dear doughty ones whom death had taken. Now sit down to the banquet and unbind thy thoughts, thy hopes to the thanes, as thy mind inspires thee.' Then was there room made in the beer-hall for the Geats all together. And there they went and sat down, the strong-hearted men, proud of their strength. And a thane waited on them, who bore in his hands the ale-cup bedecked, and he poured out the sparkling mead, while the clear-voiced bard kept singing in Hart. There was joy to the heroes, and a very great gathering of Danes and of Geats.

8

Spake then Unferth, the son of Ecglaf, who sat at the feet of the Lord of the Danes and opened a quarrel. (For the journey of Beowulf, of the brave sea-farer, was vexation to him, for he could not brook that ever any other man than he himself should obtain greater fame in all the earth.)

'What!' said he, 'art thou that Beowulf who didst contend with Breca, and strovest for the mastery in swimming o'er wide seas, when ye two for pride were searching the waves and for foolish boasting risked your lives in the deep waters? No man could dissuade you from that sorrowful journey, neither friend nor foe, when ye two swam in the sea, when ye two enfolded the waves with your arms and measured the sea-ways and brandished your arms as you glided o'er the ocean. The sea boiled with waves the wintry whelming. And for seven nights long ye were toiling in the stress of seas. But he o'erpowered thee in swimming, for greater strength had he. Then at the morning tide the sea bore him up to the land of the Heathoremes. Thence he was seeking the friend of his people his own dear country, the land of the Brondings, the fair city of refuge, where he had his own folk, and a city and rings. The son of Beanstan soothly fulfilled his boasting against thee. So do I deem it a worse matter, though thou art everywhere doughty in the rush of battle and grim warfare, if thou shalt be daring to bide near Grendel a night-long space.'

Then Beowulf spake, the son of Ecgtheow: 'What! my friend Unferth, drunken with beer, many things thou art saying about that Breca and talkest of his journey. But soothly I tell thee that I had the greater strength in that swimming, and endurance in the waves. We two agreed when we were youngsters, and boasted (for we were both still in the days of our youth) that we in the ocean would be risking our lives. And so in deed we did. We had a naked sword hard in our hands when we were swimming. We two were thinking to guard us 'gainst whale fishes. Nor over the sea-waves might he be floating a whit far from me, more quickly on the waters. Then we together were in the sea for the space of five nights until the flood, the boiling waters drove us asunder.

And the coldest of weather, and the darkening night, and a wind from
the north battle-grim turned against us, and rough were the waves. And
the mind of the mere-fishes was stirred when my shirt of mail that was
hand-locked gave to me help against the foe. The decorated battle-robe
lay on my breast all adorned with gold, and the doomèd and dire foe
drew to the bottom, and fast he had me grim in his grip. Still to me
was granted that I reached to the monster with the point of my sword.
And the mighty sea-deer carried off the battle-rush through my hand.'

9

'So then evil-doers did often oppress me. And I served them with my dear sword as was most fitting. Not at all of the feasting had they any joy. Evil destroyers sat round the banquet at the bottom of the sea, that they might seize me. But in the morning, wounded by my sword, they lay up on the foreshore, put to sleep by my weapon so that they hindered no more the faring of the sea-goers. Light came from the eastward, the bright beacon of God. The waves grew less that I could catch sight of the sea-nesses, the windy walls. Weird often saveth the earl that is undoomed when his courage is doughty. Nevertheless it happened that I slew with my sword nine of the sea-monsters. Nor have I heard under vault of heaven of a harder night-struggle, nor of a more wretched man on the sea-streams. Still I escaped from the grasp of the foes, with my life, and weary of the journey. When the sea bore me up, on the flood tide, on the welling of waves, to the land of the Finns. Nor have I heard concerning thee of any such striving or terror of swords. Breca never yet, nor either of you two, did such a deed with shining sword in any battle-gaming (not that I will boast of this too much), yet wast thou the slayer of thy brother, thy chief kinsman. And for this in hell shalt thou suffer a curse, though thy wit be doughty. And soothly I tell thee, O son of Eglaf, that Grendel that hateful monster never had done such terrors to thy life and humiliation in Hart if thy mind and thy soul were as battle-fierce as thou thyself dost say. But he has found that he needed not to fear the feud the terrible sword-thrust of your people the Danes. He taketh forced toll, and spareth none of the Danish people, but joyfully wageth war, putteth them to sleep and feedeth on them, and expecteth no fight from the Danes. But I shall ere long offer him in war the strength and the courage of the Geats. Let him go who can to the mead hall proudly when morning light shall shine from the south, another day over the children of men.'

Then in the hall the giver of rings was grey-haired and battle-brave. The Prince of the Danes was hopeful of help. The guardian of the folk fixed on Beowulf his firm-purposed thought. There was laughter 'mong heroes, din resounded, and words were winsome. Wealtheow went forth, the Queen of Hrothgar, mindful of kinship and decked out in gold, she greeted Beowulf in the hall. And then the lovely wife first proffered the goblet to the Lord of the East Danes, and bade him be blithe at the beer-drinking, he who was dear to all his people. And gladly he took the banquet and hall-cup, he the victorious King. The lady of the Helmings[14] went round about every one of the youthful warriors, and proffered the costly cup, until the time came that the ring-adorned Queen, most excellent in spirit, bore the mead-cup then to Beowulf. She, the wise in words, greeted the Geats and gave thanks to God that she had her desire that she might trust in any earl for help against such crimes. He gladly received it, he the battle-fierce warrior, from the hand of Wealtheow, and then began singing, inspired by a warlike spirit.

Beowulf spake, the son of Ecgtheow: 'I had intended at once to work out the will of this your people when I set forth over the sea and sat in my sea-boat with the troop of my people, or that I would fall in the slaughter fast in the fiend's grip. I shall yet acquit myself as befitteth an earl, or in the mead-hall await my last day.' And well the lady liked the words, the boasting of the Geat. And that lovely queen went all decked out in gold to sit by her lord. Then mighty words were spoken in the hall as before, by the people in joyance and the noise of the victors, until the son of Healfdene[15] straightway would be seeking his evening rest. And he knew that a battle was doomed in the high hall to the monster when no longer they could see the light of the sun, or darkening night came stalking over all the shapes of shadows. The troop of warriors rose up, the Lord greeted the other, Hrothgar greeted Beowulf, and wished him good health and the warding of that wine-hall, and he spake the word: 'Since the time that I could lift my hand or my shield, never have I given the mighty hall of the Danes into the care of any, except now to thee. Have now and hold thou this best of houses, be thou mindful of honour, and show thyself courageous, and wakeful 'gainst foes. Nor shalt thou lack joy if thou escapest from that brave work with life.'

10

Then Hrothgar departed with his troop of heroes, he the Prince of the Scyldings; out of Hall went he, for the battle-chieftain would be seeking out Wealtheow his Queen, that they might go to rest. The glory of kings had appointed a hall-ward, as men say, against Grendel. A thane was in waiting on the Prince of the Danes, and his watch was keeping against the giant. The Lord of the Geats readily trusted the proud strength, the favour of God. Then doffed he the iron coat of mail and his helmet from his head, and gave his sword bedecked, the choicest of weapons, to a thane that was serving, and bade him to hold ready his armour. Then the good man spoke some words of boasting: 'I reck not myself meaner in war-powers and works of battle than Grendel doth himself. For I will not with sword put him to sleep and be taking his life away, though well I might do it. He knows not of good things, that he may strike me, or hew my shield, though brave he may be in hostile working—but we two by right will forbear the sword if he dare be seeking warfare without weapon, and then God all-knowing, the holy Lord, shall adjudge the glory on whichever side He may think meet.' Then the bold in fight got him to rest, and the pillow received the head of the earl, and many a keen sea-warrior lay down on his bed in the hall about him. None of them thought that he thence would ever seek another dear home, folk or free city where he was a child; for they had heard that fell death had taken, ere this too many, in that wine-hall, of the people of the Danes. But the Lord gave weavings of war-speed to the people of the Geats, both comfort and help. So that they all overcame their enemies through the craft of one man and by his might only. And truly it is said that God Almighty doth wield for ever the race of men. Then came in the wan night the shadow-goer gliding. Warriors were sleeping when they should have been keeping guard over that palace; all save one only. It was well known to men that their constant foe could not draw them into shadowy places when the Creator was unwilling. But he, ever wakeful, in angry mood, and fiercely indignant against the foe, was waiting the issue.

11

Then came Grendel, stalking from the moors among the misty hill-slopes, and he bore God's anger. And the wicked scather of human kind fully intended to ensnare a certain one in the high hall. So he wended his way under the welkin to where he knew that the best of wine-halls, the gold-hall of man, was adorned with gold plating. Nor was that the first time that he sought out the home of Hrothgar. Nor ever in former or later days did he find a harder welcome from hall-thanes. Then the creature bereft of all joy came to the great hall, and the door, strongly bound with fire-bands, soon sprang open at his touch. And the evil-minded one in his fury burst open the door of the palace. And soon after this the enemy, angry in mind, was treading o'er the doomèd floor. And a fearsome light streamed forth from his eyes likest to a flame. And he could see many a warrior in that palace, a troop of peace-lovers asleep together, a company of kinsmen, and he laughed aloud. Then the terrible monster fully intended to cut off from life every one of them there, when he was expecting abundance of meat. But that fate was not yet, that he should lay hold of any more of human kind after that night.

Then did Beowulf, kinsman of Hygelac, see the dire distress, how the wicked scather would fare with sudden grip. Nor did the monster think to delay, but at the first he quickly laid hold of a sleeping warrior, and tore him to pieces all unawares, and bit at the flesh and drank the streaming blood, and devoured huge pieces of flesh. And soon he had eaten up both feet and hands of the man he had killed. Then he stepped up to the great-hearted warrior[16] where he lay on the bed, and took him in his hands. He reached out his hand against the enemy, and quickly received him with hostile intent, and sat upon his arm. The Keeper of crimes soon was finding that he never had met in all the quarters of the earth amongst other men a greater hand-grip. And in mind and heart he was fearful, and eager to be gone and to flee away into darkness to seek the troop of devils. But that was not his fate, as it had been in days of yore. Then the good kinsman of Hygelac remembered the evening talk, and stood upright and laid hold upon him. His fingers burst. The giant was going forth, but the earl stepped after. The famous one intended to escape more widely, howsoever he might, and to flee on his way thence to the sloping hollows of the fens. That journey was sorrowful, which the harmful scather took to Hart. The lordly hall resounded. And great terror there was to all the Danes, the castle-dwellers, to each of the brave. And both the mighty guardians were fiercely angry. The hall resounded. Then was it great wonder that the wine-hall withstood the bold fighters, and that it fell not to the earth, that fair earth-dwelling. But very firm it was standing, cunningly shaped by craft of the smith, within and without. Then on the floor was many a mead-bench, as I have heard tell, decked out with gold, where the fierce ones were striving. Nor did the wise Danes formerly suppose that any man could break down a hall so noble and decorated with antlers, or cunningly destroy it, unless the bosom of flame swallowed it up in smoke. The roaring went up now enough. And an awful terror came to the North Danes, to each one of those who heard weeping from the ramparts, the enemy of God singing a fierce song, a song that was empty of victory, and the captive of hell lamenting his sorrow. For he that was strongest of men in strength held him fast on the day of his life.

12

The Prince of earls would not at all let go alive the murderous comer, nor did he count his life as of use to any of the peoples. And many an earl of Beowulf's brandished the old heirloom, and were wishful to defend the life of their far-famed liege-lord, if they might do so. And they knew not, when they entered the battle, they the hard-thinking ones, the battle-men, and they thought to hew on all sides seeking out his spirit, that not any choice iron over the earth nor any battle weapon could be greeting the foe, but that he had forsworn all victorious weapons and swords. And miserable should be his passing on the day of this life, and the hostile sprite should journey far into the power of devils. Then he found out that, he who did crimes long before this with mirthful mind to human kind, he who was a foe to God, that his body would not last out; but the proud kinsman of Hygelac had him in his hands. And each was loathsome to the other while he lived. The terrible monster, sore with wounds was waiting. The gaping wound was seen on his shoulder. His sinews sprang open; and the bone-lockers burst. And great victory was given to Beowulf. Thence would Grendel, mortally wounded, flee under the fen-slopes to seek out a joyless dwelling. The more surely he knew he had reached the end of his life, the number of his days. Joy befell all the Danes after the slaughter-rush. So he had cleansed the hall of Hrothgar—he who had come from far, the proud and stout-hearted one, and saved them from strife. He rejoiced in the night-work and in the glorious deeds. His boast he had fulfilled, this leader of the Geats, which he made to the East Danes, and likewise made good all the distresses and the sorrows which they suffered of yore from the foe, and which through dire need they had to endure, of distresses not a few. And when the battle-brave man laid down the hand, the arm and shoulder under the wide roof, that was the manifest token.

13

Then in the morning, as I have heard say, was many a battle-warrior round about the gift-hall. Came the folk-leaders from far and from near along the wide ways to look at the marvel. Nor did his passing seem a thing to grieve over to any of the warriors of those who were scanning the track of the glory-less wight, how weary in mind he had dragged along his life-steps, on the way thence doomed and put to flight, and overcome in the fight at the lake of the sea-monsters. There was the sea boiling with blood, the awful surge of waves all mingled with hot gore. The death-doomèd one dyed the lake when void of joys he laid down his life in the fen for refuge. And hell received him. Thence after departed the old companions, likewise many a young one from the joyous journeys, proud from the lake to ride on mares, the youths on their horses. And there was the glory of Beowulf proclaimed. And many a one was saying that no man was a better man, no, none in the whole wide world under arch of the sky, of all the shield-bearers, neither south nor north, by the two seas. Nor a whit did they blame in the least their friend and lord, the glad Hrothgar; for he was a good king.

Meanwhile the famed in battle let the fallow mares leap and go faring forth to the contest, wherever the earth-ways seemed fair unto them and well known for their choiceness: and the thane of the king, he who was laden with many a vaunt, and was mindful of songs, and remembered a host of very many old sagas, he found other words, but bound by the truth. And a man began wisely to sing the journey of Beowulf, and to tell skilful tales with speeding that was good, and to interchange words. He told all that ever he had heard concerning Sigmund,[17] with his deeds of courage, and much that is unknown, the strife of Waelsing; and the wide journeys which the children of men knew not at all, the feud and the crimes, when Fitela was not with him, when he would be saying any of such things, the uncle to the nephew, for always they were comrades in need at all the strivings. They had laid low very many of the giant's race by means of the sword. And after his death-day a not little fame sprang up for Sigmund when he, the hard in battle, killed the worm, the guardian of the hoard. He alone the child

of the Atheling, hazarded a fearful deed, under the grey stone. Nor
was Fitela with him. Still it happened to him that his sword pierced
through the wondrous worm, and it stood in the wall, that doughty
iron, and the dragon was dead. And so this monster had gained strength
in that going so that he might enjoy the hoard of rings by his own
doom. He loaded the sea-boat and bore the bright treasures on to the
ship's bosom, he the son of Waels. The worm melted hot. He was of
wanderers the most widely famous in deeds of courage, amongst men,
the protector of warriors. He formerly throve thus. Then the warfare
of Heremod[18] was waning, his strength and his courage, and he was
betrayed among the giants into the hands of the foes, and sent quickly
away. And too long did whelming sorrow vex his soul. He was a source
of care to his people, to all the nobles, and many a proud churl often
was lamenting in former times the way of life of the stout-hearted, they
who trusted him for the bettering of bales, that the child of their lord
should always be prospering, and succeed to his father's kingdom, and
hold the folk, the hoard and city of refuge, the kingdom of heroes, the
country of the Danes. But Beowulf Hygelac's kinsman was fairer to all
men; but crime assailed Heremod.[19]

Sometimes they passed along the fallow streets contending on
mares. Then came the light of morning and hastened forth. And many
a stiff-minded messenger went to the high hall to see the rare wonder.
Likewise the King himself, the ward of the hoard of rings, came treading
all glorious and with a great suite, forth from the bridal bower, and
choice was his bearing, and his Queen with him passed along the way
to the Mead-hall with a troop of maidens.

14

Hrothgar spake. He went to the hall and stood on the threshold and saw the steep roof all decked out with gold and the hand of Grendel. 'Let thanks be given quickly to God for this sight,' said he. 'Often I waited for the loathsome one, for the snares of Grendel. May God always work wonder after wonder, He the Guardian of glory. It was not long ago that I expected not a bettering of any woes for ever, when, doomed to blood, this best of all houses stood all stained with gore. Now has this Hero done a deed, through the power of the Lord, which none of us formerly could ever perform with all our wisdom. Lo! any woman who gave birth to such a son among human kind, may say, if she yet live, that the Creator was gracious unto her in bearing of children. Now, O Beowulf, I will love thee in heart as my son. Hold well to this new peace. Nor shall there be any lack of joys to thee in the world, over which I have power. Full oft I for less have meted out rewards and worshipful gifts to a meaner warrior, one weaker in strife. Thou hast framed for thyself mighty deeds, so that thy doom liveth always and for ever. May the All-wielder ever yield thee good as He now doth.'

Beowulf spake, the son of Ecgtheow: 'We framed to fight that brave work with much favour, and hazarded a deed of daring and the might of the unknown. I quickly gave you to see the monster himself the enemy in his fretted armour ready to fall. I thought to twist him quickly with hard grip on a bed of slaughter so that he should lie in the throes of death, because of my hand-grip, unless he should escape with his body. But I could not cut off his going when the Creator willed it not. I cleft him not readily, that deadly fiend. He was too strong on his feet. Nevertheless he left behind his hand as a life protection to show the track, his arm and his shoulders. But not by any means thus did that wretched creature get any help, nor by that did the evil-doer, brought low by sin, live any longer. But sorrow hath him in its fatal grip closely encompassed with baleful bands. There shall a man covered with sins be biding a mickle doom as the shining Creator will prescribe.'

Then was the man silent, the son of Ecglaf, in his boasting speech about deeds of battle, when the Athelings looked at the hand high up

on the roof, by the craft of the earl, and the fingers of the foe, there
before each one. And each of the places of the nails was likest to steel,
the claw of the heathen, the uncanny claw of the battle warrior. Every
one was saying that no very good iron, of any of the brave ones, would
touch him at all, that would bear away thence the bloody battle-hand
of the monster.

15

Then was it bidden that Hart should be decked by their hands on the inside. And many there were of the men and wives who adorned that wine-hall the guest-chamber. And the tapestries shone along the walls brocaded with gold; many a wonderful sight for every man who stareth upon them. And that bright dwelling was greatly marred, though within it was fast bound with iron, yet the door-hinges had sprung apart. The roof alone escaped all safe and sound when the monster turned to flight, despairing of life and doomed for his crimes. Nor will it be easy to escape from that fate, whosoever may try to, but he shall get by strife the ready place of the children of men of the soul-bearers, who dwell upon earth, by a fate that cannot be escaped where his body shall sleep after the banquet fast in the tomb.

Then was the time for Healfdene's son to go into the hall, when the King himself would partake of the banquet. Nor have I ever heard tell that any people in greater numbers bore themselves better about their treasure-giver. And the wealthy ones sat down on the bench and rejoiced in their feeding. And full courteously their kinsmen took many a mead-cup, they the stout-hearted Hrothgar and Hrothulf in the high hall. And within was Hart filled with friends. And by no means were the Danes the while framing treacheries. Then the son of Healfdene gave to Beowulf the golden banner, the decorated staff banner as a reward for his conquest, and the helm and the byrny. And many a one saw the youth bear in front the bejewelled sword. Beowulf took the cup in the hall. Nor did he need to be ashamed of the fee-gift in the presence of warriors. Nor have I heard tell of many men giving to others on any ale-bench, four gifts gold-decked, in friendlier fashion. The outside rim wound with wires gave protection to the head on the outer side around the crown of the helmet. So that many an heirloom[20] could not hurt fiercely the helmet that was hardened by being plunged in cold water when the shield-warrior should attack the angry one. The Protector of earls commanded eight horses to be brought in under the barriers, with bridles gold plated. And a varicoloured saddle was fixed upon one of them, decked out with treasures, and this was the battle-seat of the high

King when the son of Healfdene would be doing the sword-play. Never in the van did it fail the warrior so widely kenned when the helmets were falling. Then the Prince of the Danes gave to Beowulf the wielding of them both, of horses and weapons; and bade him well enjoy them. And thus in manly fashion the famous chieftain, the treasure-guardian of heroes, rewarded the battle onslaught with horses and treasures so as no man can blame them, whoever will be saying rightly the truth.

16

Then the Lord of earls as he sat on the mead-bench gave glorious gifts to each one of those who had fared with Beowulf over the ocean-ways, and heirlooms they were; and he bade them atone for that one with gold whom formerly Grendel had wickedly killed as he would have done more of them unless Almighty God and the spirit of Beowulf had withstood Weird. The Creator ruleth all of human kind, as still He is doing. And good understanding is always the best thing, and forethought of mind. And he who long enjoys here the world in these strife-days, shall be biding both pleasant and loathsome fate. Then was there clamour and singing together in the presence of the battle-prince of Healfdene, and the harp was sounded and a song often sung, when Hrothgar's scop would tell forth the hall-mirth as he sat on the mead-bench.

'When Fear was befalling the heirs of Finn,[21] the hero of the Half-Danes, and Hnaef of the Danes must fall in the slaughter of the Frisian People. Not in the least did Hildeburh need to be praising the troth of the Jutes. For sinlessly was she deprived of her dear ones in the play of swords of children and brothers. By fate they fell, wounded by arrows. And she was a sad woman. Nor without reason did the daughter of Hoc[22] mourn their doom. When morning light came, and she could see under the sky the murder of her kinsmen where she before in the world had the greatest of joy. For warfare took away all the thanes of Finn except a mere remnant, so that he could not in the place where they met fight any warfare at all with Hengest, nor seize from the Prince's thane the woful leavings by fighting. But they offered him terms, so that they all made other room for them on the floor, and gave them halls and a high seat that they might have half the power with the children of the Jutes; and the son of Folcwalda[23] honoured the Danes every day with fee-givings, and bestowed rings on the troop of Hengest, yea, even great treasures plated with gold, so that he would be making the kin of the Frisians bold in the beer-hall. Then they swore on both sides a treaty of peace. Finn swore with Hengest and all without strife that he held in honour the woful remnant by the doom of the wise men, and that no man there by word or work should break the treaty, or ever annul it through treacherous cunning, though they followed the slayers of their Ring-giver, all bereft of their lord as was needful for them. But if any one of the Frisians by daring speech should bring to mind the murderous hate between them, then should the edge of the sword avenge it. Then sworn was that oath, and massive gold was lifted up from the hoard. Then was Hnaef, the best of the warriors, of the bold Danes, ready on the funeral pyre. And the blood-stained shirt of mail was easily seen, the golden boar, in the midst of the flame, the iron-hard boar,[24] and many an Atheling destroyed by wounds. Some fell on the field of death. Then Hildeburh commanded her very own son to be thrust in the flames of the pyre of Hnaef, his body to be burned and be put in the fire. And great was the moaning of the mother for her son, and dirge-like lamenting as the warrior ascended. And the greatest of slaughter-fires wound its way upwards towards the welkin and roared before the cavern. Heads were melting, wounds burst asunder. Then blood sprang forth from the wounds of the body. Flame swallowed all, that most cruel of ghosts, of both of those folk whom battle destroyed. Their life was shaken out.

17

'Then the warriors went forth to visit the dwellings which were bereft of friends, and to look upon the land of the Frisians, the homesteads and the high town. And Hengest was still dwelling with Finn, that slaughter-stained winter, all bravely without strife. And he thought on the homeland, though he could not be sailing his ringed ship over the waters. The sea boiled with storm and waged war with the wind. And winter locked up the ice-bound waves till yet another year came in the court, as still it doth, which ever guards the seasons, and the glory-bright weather. Then winter was scattered, and fair was the bosom of the earth.[25] And the wanderer strove to go, the guest from the court. And much more he thought of vengeance for the feud than of the sea-voyage, as to how he could bring about an angry encounter, for he bore in mind the children of the Jutes. And so he escaped not the lot of mortals when Hunlafing did on his arm the best of swords, the flashing light of the battle, whose edge was well known to the Jutes. And dire sword-bale after befel the fierce-minded Finn, even in his very own home, when Guthlaf and Oslaf lamented the grim grip of war and the sorrow after sea-journeys, and were charging him with his share in the woes. Nor could he hold back in his own breast his fluttering soul. Then again was the hall adorned with the bodies of foemen, and Finn was also slain, the King with his troop, and the Queen was taken. And the warriors of the Danes carried to the ships all the belongings of the earth-king, such as they could find in the homestead of Finn, of ornaments and jewels. They bore away also the noble wife Hildeburh down to the sea away to the Danes, and led her to her people.'

So a song was sung, a lay of the gleemen, and much mirth there was and great noise from the benches. And cup-bearers offered wine from wondrous vessels. Then came forth Queen Wealtheow in her golden circlet, where the two good men were sitting, the uncle and his nephew. And still were they in peace together, and each true to the other. Likewise Unferth the Spokesman sat there at the foot of the Lord of the Danes. And each of them trusted Unferth's good heart and that he had a great soul, though he was not loyal to his kinsmen at the sword-play.

Then spake the Queen of the Danes: 'Take this cup, O my liege lord, thou giver of rings. Be thou right joyful, thou gold-friend to men; do thou speak mild words to the Geats, as a man should be doing. Be glad of thy Geats and mindful of gifts. Now thou hast peace both near and far. There is one who told me that thou wouldst have the battle-hero for thy son. Now Hart is all cleansed, the bright hall of rings. Enjoy whilst thou mayest many rewards, and leave to thy kinsmen both folk and a kingdom when thou shalt go forth to look on eternity. I know my glad Hrothulf[26] will hold in honour this youth if thou, O Hrothgar the friend of the Danes, dost leave the world earlier than he. I ween that he will yield good to our children if he remembers all that has passed—how we two worshipfully showed kindness to him in former days when he was but a child.' Then she turned to the bench where were her sons Hrothric and Hrothmund and the children of heroes, the youths all together. There sat the good man Beowulf of the Geats, by the two brothers.

18

And the cup was borne to them, and a friendly invitation given to them in words, and twisted gold was graciously proffered him, two arm-ornaments, armour and rings, and the greatest of neck-rings of which I heard tell anywhere on earth. Ne'er heard I of better hoard jewels of heroes under the sky, since Hama carried away the Brosinga-men[27] to the bright city, ornaments and treasure vessel. It was he who fled from the cunning plots of Eormanric[28] and chose eternal gain. Hygelac of the Geats next had the ring, he who was the grandson of Swerting, when under the standard he protected the treasure and defended the plunder. And Weird carried him off when he, because of pride suffered woes, the feud with the Frisians. Then carried he the jewels, the precious stones over the sea, he who was the ruling prince, and he fell under shield; and the life of the king and the coat of mail and ring together came into possession of the Franks. And worse warriors plundered the slaughter after the war. And the corpses of the Geats held the field of death. The hall resounded with noise when Wealtheow spake these words in the midst of the court:

'Enjoy this ring, dearest Beowulf, and use this coat of mail, these national treasures, and good luck befall thee! Declare thyself a good craftsman, and be to these boys gentle in teaching, and I will be mindful of thy guerdon for that thou hast so acted that men will esteem thee far and near for ever and ever, even as widely as the sea doth encompass the windy earth-walls. Be a noble Atheling as long as thou livest. I give thee many treasures. Be thou kindly in deed to my sons, joyful as thou art. For here is each earl true to his fellow, and mild of mood, and faithful to his liege-lord. Thanes are gentle, the people all ready. O ye warriors who have drunk deep, do as I tell you.' She went to the seat where was a choice banquet, and the men drank wine. They knew not Weird, the Fate that was grim, as it had befallen many an earl.

Then evening came on, and Hrothgar betook him to his own quarters, the Prince to his resting-place, and a great number of earls kept guard o'er the palace as often they had done in former days. They laid bare the bench-board and spread it over with beds and bolsters. And one of the beer-servants eager and fated went to his bed on the floor. And they set at his head war-shields, that were bright. And over the Atheling, there on the bench was easily seen the towering helmet and the ringed byrny, the glorious spear. It was their wont to be ready for war both at home and in battle, at whatever time their lord had need of them. The season was propitious.

19

Then they sank down to sleep. And sorely some of them paid for their evening repose, as full often it had happened to them since Grendel came to the gold-hall and did evil, until an end was made of him, death after sins. It was easily seen and widely known to men that an avenger survived the loathsome one, for a long time after the war-sorrow. A woman, the mother of Grendel, a terrible wife, bore in mind her woes. She who was fated to dwell in the awful lake in the cold streams since Cain became a sword-slayer to his only brother, his father's son. He then went forth marked for the murder, and fled from human joys and dwelt in the waste. And thence he awoke many a fatal demon. And Grendel was one of them, the hateful fierce wolf, who found the man wide awake awaiting the battle. And there was the monster at grips with him, yet he remembered the main strength the wide and ample gift which God gave to him, and trusted in the favour of the Almighty for himself, for comfort and help by which he vanquished the enemy and overcame the hell-sprite. Then he departed abject, bereft of joy, to visit the death-place, he the enemy of mankind.

But his mother, greedy and sad in mind would be making a sorrowful journey that she might avenge the death of her son. She came then to Hart, where the Ring-Danes were asleep in that great hall. Then soon there came misfortune to the earls when the mother of Grendel entered the chamber. Yet less was the terror, even by so much as the craft of maidens, the war-terror of a wife,[29] is less than that of men beweaponed—when the sword hard bound and forged by the hammer, and stained with blood, cuts the boar on the helmet of the foe with its edge. Then in the hall, the hard edge was drawn, the sword over the seats, and many a broad shield, heaved up fast by the hand. And no one heeded the helmet nor the broad shield when terror seized upon them. She was in great haste, she would go thence her life to be saving when she was discovered. Quickly she had seized one of the Athelings fast in her grip when forth she was fleeing away to the fen-land. He was to Hrothgar the dearest of heroes, in the number of his comrades by the two seas, a powerful shield-warrior, whom she killed as he slumbered, a youth of renown. Beowulf was not there. To another the place was assigned after the treasure-gift had been bestowed on the famous Geat. Then a great tumult was made in Hart, and with bloodshed she had seized the well-known hand of Grendel her son. And care was renewed in all the dwellings. Nor was that a good exchange that they on both sides should be buying with the lives of their friends.

Then was the wise King, the hoar battle-warrior, rough in his mood when he came to know that the dearest of his chief thanes was dead and bereft of life. And Beowulf quickly was fetched into the bower, he, the man all victorious. And at the dawning went one of the earls, a noble champion, he and his comrades, where the proud man was waiting, to see whether the All-wielder will ever be causing a change after woe-spells. And the battle-worthy man went along the floor with his band of followers (the hall wood[30] was resounding) so that he greeted the wise man with words, the Lord of the Danes, and asked him if he had had a quiet night in spite of the pressing call.

20

Hrothgar spake, he the Lord of the Danes: 'Ask not after our luck, for sorrow is renewed to the folk of the Danes. Aeschere is dead, the elder brother of Yrmenlaf; he was my councillor and my rune-teller,[31] my shoulder-companion when we in the battle protected our heads; when troops were clashing and helmets were crashing. He was what an earl ought to be, a very good Atheling. Such a man was Aeschere. And a wandering slaughter-guest was his hand-slayer, in Hart. I know not whither that dire woman exulting in carrion, and by her feeding made famous, went on her journeys. She was wreaking vengeance for the feud of thy making when thou killedst Grendel but yesternight, in a violent way, with hard grips, because all too long he was lessening and destroying my people. He fell in the struggle, gave his life as a forfeit; and now comes another, a mighty man-scather, to avenge her son, and the feud hath renewed as may seem a heavy heart-woe to many a thane who weeps in his mind over the treasure-giver. Now lieth low the hand which availed you well, for every kind of pleasure. I heard land-dwellers, and hall-counsellors, and my people, say that they saw two such monstrous March-steppers,[32] alien-sprites, holding the moorland. And one of them was in the likeness of a woman as far as they could tell; the other, shapen wretchedly, trod the path of exiles in the form of a man, except that he was greater than any other man, he whom in former days the earth-dwellers called by name Grendel. They knew not his father, whether any secret sprite was formerly born of him. They kept guard over the hidden land, and the wolf-slopes, the windy nesses, the terrible fen-path where the mountain streams rush down under mists of the nesses, the floods under the earth. And it is not farther hence than the space of a mile where standeth the lake, over which are hanging the frosted trees, their wood fast by the roots, and shadowing the water. And there every night one may see dread wonders, fire on the flood. And there liveth not a wise man of the children of men who knoweth well the ground. Nevertheless the heath-stepper, the strong-horned hart, when pressed by the hounds seeketh that woodland, when put to flight from afar, ere on the hillside, hiding his head he gives up his life.[33]

'Nor is that a canny place. For thence the surge of waters riseth up wan to the welkin when stirred by the winds, the loathsome weather, until the heaven darkens and skies weep. Now is good counsel depending on thee alone. Thou knowest not the land, the terrible places where thou couldest find the sinful man; seek it if thou darest. I will reward thee for the feud with old world treasures so I did before, with twisted gold, if thou comest thence, on thy way.'

21

Beowulf spake, the son of Ecgtheow: 'Sorrow not, O wise man. It is better for each one to avenge his friend, when he is much mourning. Each one of us must wait for the end of his world-life. Let him work who may, ere the doom of death come; that is afterwards best for the noble dead. Arise, O ward of the kingdom. Let us go forth quickly to trace out the going of Grendel's kinswoman. I bid thee do it. For neither in the bosom of the earth, nor in forests of the mountains, nor by the ways of the sea, go where she will, shall she escape into safety. Do thou this day be patient in every kind of trouble as I also hope to be.' The old man leapt up and gave thanks to God, the mighty Lord, for the words of Beowulf.

Then was bridled a horse for Hrothgar, a steed with twisted hair, and as a wise prince he went forth in splendid array. The troop of shield-warriors marched along. And the traces were widely seen in the forest-ways, the goings of Grendel's mother over the ground. Forwards she had gone over the mirky moorlands, and had borne in her grasp, bereft of his soul, the best of the thanes who were wont to keep watch over Hrothgar's homestead. Then Beowulf, the Atheling's child, stepped o'er the steep and stony slopes and the narrow pathways, and the straitened single tracks, an unknown way, by the steep nesses, and by many a sea-monster's cavern. And one of the wise men went on before to seek out the path, until all at once he found some mountain trees, overhanging the grey stones, a forest all joyless. And underneath was a water all bloodstained and troubled. And a grievous thing it was for all the Danes to endure, for the friends of the Scyldings,[34] and for many a thane, and distressful to all the earls, when they came upon the head of Aeschere on the cliffs above the sea. The flood boiled with blood and with hot gore (the folk looked upon it). And at times the horn sounded a battle-song ready prepared.

All the troop sat down. And many kinds of serpents they saw in the water, and wonderful dragons searching the sea, and on the cliff-slopes, monsters of the ocean were lying at full length, who at the morning tide often make a woful journey on the sail-path; and snakes and wild

beasts they could see also. And these living things fell down on the
path all bitter and angry when they perceived the noise, and the blast
of the war-horn. And the Prince of the Geats killed one of them with
his bow and arrows and ended his wave-strife, and he was in the sea,
slower at swimming as death swept him away. And on the waves by
fierce battle hard pressed, and with boar-spears savagely barbed, the
wondrous sea-monster was assailed in the struggle and drawn up on the
headland. And men were looking at the awful stranger. And Beowulf
put on him his armour, that was fitting for an earl, and by no means
did he lament over his life, for the hand-woven coat of mail, which was
ample and of many colours, was destined to explore the deeps, and
knew well how to defend his body, so that neither battle-grip nor the
hostile grasp of the treacherous one might scathe breast or life; and
the white helmet thereof warded his head, that which was destined to
search out the bottom of the sea and the welter of waters, and which
was adorned with treasures and encircled with noble chains, wondrously decked and set round with boar-images, as in days of yore a
weapon-smith had made it for him, so that no brand nor battle-sword
could bite him. And by no means was that the least of aids in battle that
the Spokesman of Hrothgar[35] lent him at need, even the hilted sword
which was called Hrunting. And it was one of the ancient treasures.
Its edge was of iron, and poison-tipped, and hardened in battle-sweat.
And never did it fail in the fight any man who brandished it in his
hands, or who dared to go on fearful journeys, to the field of battle.
And that was not the first time that it was to do deeds of courage. And
Unferth did not think, he the kinsman of Ecglaf, crafty of strength,
of what he formerly had said[36] when drunken with wine, he had lent
that weapon to a braver sword-warrior. He himself durst not risk his
life in the stress of the waters and do a glorious deed. And thereby he
lost his doom of famous deeds. But thus was it not with that other,
for he had got himself ready for the battle.

22

Beowulf spake, the son of Ecgtheow: 'O kinsman of Healfdene,[37] thou far-famed and proud prince, thou gold-friend of men, now that eager I am for this forth-faring, bethink thee now of what we two were speaking together, that if I should lose my life through helping thee in thy need, thou wouldst be always to me in the place of a father after my death. Be thou a guardian to my kinsmen, my thanes, and my hand comrades, if battle should take me. And dear Hrothgar, send thou the gifts, which thou didst give me, to Hygelac. And the Lord of the Geats, the son of Hrethel, when he looks on the treasure and perceives the gold, will see that I found a giver of rings, one good and open-handed, and that while I could, I enjoyed the treasures. And do thou let Unferth, the man who is far-famed, have the old heirloom, the curiously wrought sword with its wave-like device, with its hard edge. I work out my fate with Hrunting, or death shall seize me.'

After these words the Lord of the Weder-Geats courageously hastened, and by no means would he wait for an answer. The whelming sea received the battle-hero. And it was a day's while before he could see the bottom of the sea. And very soon the fierce and eager one who had ruled the expanse of the floods for a hundred years, she, the grim and greedy, saw that a man was searching out from above the dwelling of strange monsters. Then she made a grab at him, and closed on the warrior with dire embrace. But not at first did she scathe his body, safe and sound. The ring surrounded it on the outside, so that she could not pierce the coat of mail or the interlaced war-shirt with loathsome finger. Then the sea-wolf, when she came to the bottom of the sea, bore the Ring-Prince towards her house so that he might not, though he was so strong in soul, wield any weapon; and many a wonder oppressed him in the depths, many a sea-beast broke his war-shirt with his battle-tusks, and monsters pursued him.

Then the earl saw that he was in he knew not what hall of strife, where no water scathed him a whit, nor could the sudden grip of the flood touch him because of the roof-hall. He saw, too, a firelight, a bright pale flame shining. Then the good man caught sight of the

she-wolf, that monstrous wife, down in the depths of the sea. And he
made a mighty rush with his sword. Nor did his hand fail to swing it
so that the ringed mail on her head sang a greedy death-song. Then
Beowulf the stranger discovered that the battle-blade would not bite or
scathe her life, but the edge failed the lord in his need. It had suffered
many hand-blows, and the helmet, the battle-dress of the doomed one, it
had often cut in two. That was the first time that his dear sword-treasure
failed him. Then he became resolute, and not by any means did he fail
in courage, that kinsman of Hygelac, mindful of glory. And this angry
warrior threw away the stout sword, bound round with jewels with its
wavy decorations, and with its edge of steel, so that it lay prone on the
ground; and henceforth he trusted in his strength and the hand-grasp
of might. So should a man be doing when he thinketh to be gaining
long-lasting praise in fighting, and careth not for his life. Then the
Lord of the Geats seized by the shoulder the mother of Grendel (nor
at all did he mourn over that feud), and he, the hard in battle, threw
down his deadly foe, when he was angry, so that she lay prone on the
floor. But she very quickly, with grimmest of grips, requited him a
hand-reward, and made a clutch at him. And the weary in soul, that
strongest of fighters, he the foot-warrior stumbled and fell. Then she
sat on that hall-guest, and drew forth her axe, broad and brown-edged,
and would fain be avenging the death of her child, of her only son. But
on his shoulder was the coat of mail all woven, which saved his life and
prevented the entrance of the point and the edge of the sword. And
the son of Ecgtheow, the Prince of Geats, would have surely gone a
journey under the wide earth unless that warlike coat of mail had given
him help, that hard war-net, and unless the Holy God He the cunning
Lord, and the Ruler in the heavens, had wielded the victory, and easily
decided the issue aright; then he straightway stood up.

23

Then among the weapons he caught sight of a sword, rich in victories, an old weapon of the giants, and doughty of edge, the glory of warriors. It was the choicest of weapons, and it was greater than any other man could carry to the battle-playing, and all glorious and good, a work of the giants. And he seized it by the belted hilt, he the warrior of the Danes, rough and battle-grim, and he brandished the ring-sword; and despairing of life, he angrily struck so that hardly he grasped at her neck and broke the bone-rings. And the point pierced through the doomed flesh-covering. And she fell on the floor. The sword was all bloody, and the man rejoiced in his work. Shone forth the bright flame and a light stood within, even as shineth the candle[38] from the bright heavens. And then he looked on the hall, and turned to the wall. And the thane of Hygelac, angry and resolute, heaved hard the weapon, taking it by the hilt. And the edge was not worthless to the battle-warrior, for he would be quickly requiting Grendel many a war-rush which he had done upon the West Danes, many times oftener than once when in sleeping he smote the hearth-comrade of Hrothgar, and fed on them sleeping, of the Danish folk, some fifteen men, and bore forth yet another one, that loathly prey. And well he requited him, this furious champion, when he saw the war-weary Grendel lying in death, all void of his life as formerly in Hart the battle had scathed him. His body sprang apart when after his death he suffered a stroke, a hard battle-swing; and then he struck off his head.

Right soon the proud warriors, they who with Hrothgar, looked forth on the sea, could easily see, that the surging water was all stained with blood and the grey-haired ancients spoke together about the good man, that they deemed not the Atheling would ever again come seeking the famous Prince Hrothgar glorying in victory, for it seemed unto many that the sea-wolf had destroyed him.

Then came noonday. The valiant Danes left the headland, and the gold-friend of men[39] went homeward thence. And the strangers of the Geats, sick in mind, sat and stared at the water. They knew and expected not that they would see again their liege-lord himself. Then the sword began to grow less, after the battle-sweat, into icicles of steel. And a wonder it was that it all began to melt likest to ice, when Our Father doth loosen the band of frost and unwinds the icicles, He who hath power over the seasons, He is the true God. Nor in these dwellings did the Lord of the Geats take any other treasure, though much he saw there, except the head and the hilt, decked out with jewels. The sword had melted, and the decorated weapon was burnt up. The blood was too hot, and so poisonous the alien sprite who died in that conflict. Soon Beowulf was swimming, he who formerly awaited the onset of the hostile ones in the striving, and he dived upwards through the water. And the weltering surge and the spacious lands were all cleansed when the alien sprite gave up his life and this fleeting existence.

He the stout-hearted came swimming to shore, he the Prince of the sea-men enjoying the sea-spoils, the great burden of that which he had with him. They advanced towards him and gave thanks to God, that glorious crowd of thanes, and rejoiced in their lord that they could see him once more. Then was loosed quickly from that valiant man both helmet and shield. The sea became turbid, the water under welkin, all stained with blood. And rejoicing in spirit the brave men went forth with foot-tracks and passed over the earth, the well-known pathways. And a hard task it was for each one of those proud men to bear that head away from the sea-cliff. Four of them with difficulty on a pole were bearing the head of Grendel to the gold-hall, until suddenly, valiant and battle-brave, they came to the palace, fourteen of the Geats marching along with their liege-lord who trod the field where the mead-hall stood. Then this Prince of the thanes, this man so bold of deed and honoured by Fate, this battle-dear warrior went into the hall to greet King Hrothgar. Then over the floor where warriors were drinking they bore Grendel's head, a terror to the earls and also to the Queen. And men were looking at the splendid sight of the treasures.

24

Beowulf spake, the son of Ecgtheow: 'Lo, son of Healfdene, lord of the Danes, we have brought thee this booty of the sea all joyfully, this which thou seest as a token of glory. And I hardly escaped with my life, and hazarded an arduous task of war under water. And nearly was the battle ended for me, but that God shielded me. Nor could I'm that conflict do aught with Hrunting, though the weapon was doughty. But the Ruler of men granted me to see hanging on the wall a beauteous sword mighty and ancient (often He guides those who are bereft of their comrades), and I drew the weapon. And I struck in that striving the guardian of the house when I saw my chance. Then that battle-sword that was all decked out, burned up so that blood gushed forth, the hottest of battle-sweat. But I bore off that hilt thence from the enemy, and wrought vengeance for the crimes, the deaths of the Danes, as it was fitting. And here I bid thee to take thy rest all sorrowless in Hart, with the troop of thy men and each of the thanes of thy people, the youth and the doughty ones. O Lord of the Danes, no longer need'st thou fear for them, because of earls' life-bale as before thou didst.' Then was the golden hilt, the work of the giants, given into the hand of the old warrior, the hoary battle-chief. This work of the wonder-smiths went into the possession of the Lord of the Danes after the destruction of devils; and when the man of the fierce heart, the adversary of God guilty of murder, forsook this world, it passed to the best of world-kings by the two seas, of these who in Sceden Isle dealt out treasures.

Hrothgar spake and looked upon the hilt, the old heirloom on which was written the beginning of the ancient feud since the flood, the all-embracing ocean slew the giant race, when they bore themselves presumptuously. They were a folk strangers to the eternal God, to whom the ruler gave their deserts through whelming of waters. Thus was there truly marked on the sword guards of shining gold, by means of rune-staves, set down and stated by whom that sword was wrought at the first, that choicest of weapons, with its twisted hilt, adorned with a dragon. Then spake the wise man the son of Healfdene, and

all kept silence: 'He who doeth truth and right among the folk, and
he who can recall the far-off days, he the old protector of his country
may say that this earl was well born. Thy fair fame is spread throughout the wide ways, among all peoples, O my friend Beowulf. Thou
dost hold all with patience, and might, with the proud of mind. I will
perform the compact as we two agreed. Thou shalt be a lasting aid to
thy people, a help to the heroes. Not so was Heremod[40] to the sons
of Egwela, the honour-full Danish folk.[41] For he did not become a joy
to them, but slaughter and death to the Danish people. But in a fury
he killed the table-companions his boon comrades; until he alone,
the famous chieftain, turned away from human joys. And though the
mighty God greatly exalted him by the joys of strength over all people
and rendered him help, yet a fierce hoard of hate grew up in his soul;
no rings did he give to the Danes, as the custom was; and joyless he
waited, so that he suffered troublesome striving and to his people a
long time was baleful. Do thou be learning by that example and seek
out manly virtues. I who am old in winters sing thee this song. And
a wonder is it to say how the mighty God giveth wisdom to mankind
through wideness of mind, lands, and earlship. He hath power over
all. Sometimes he letteth the thought of man of famous kith and kin
be turning to love, and giveth him earth-joys in his own country, so
that he holdeth the city of refuge among men, and giveth him to rule
over parts of the world, and very wide kingdoms, so that he himself
foolishly never thinketh of his end. He dwelleth in weal; and neither
disease nor old age doth deceive him a whit, nor doth hostile sorrow
darken his mind, nor anywhere do strife or sword-hate show themselves;
but all the world doth go as he willeth.

25

'He knoweth no evil until his share of pride wasteth and groweth, while sleepeth the guardian, the ward of his soul. And the sleep is too deep, bound up in afflictions, and the banesman draweth near who shooteth cruelly his arrows from the bow. Then in his soul under helmet is he stricken with bitter shaft. Nor can he save himself from the crooked behests of the cursed ghost. And little doth he think of that which long he hath ruled. And the enemy doth covet, nor at all doth he give in boast the plated rings, and he then forgetteth and despiseth his fate, his share of honour which God before gave him, He the Wielder of wonder. And in the end it doth happen that the body sinks fleeting and doomed to death falleth. And another succeeds thereto who joyfully distributeth gifts, the old treasure of the earl, and careth not for terrors. Guard thee against malicious hate, O my dear Beowulf, thou noblest of men, and choose for thyself that better part, eternal wisdom. Have no care for pride, O glorious champion. Now is the fame of thy strength proclaimed for a while. Soon will it be that disease or sword-edge or grasp of fire or whelming of floods or grip of sword or flight of arrow or dire old age will sever thee from strength, or the lustre of thine eyes will fail or grow dim. Then forthwith will happen that death will o'erpower thee, O thou noble man. Thus have I for fifty years held sway over the Ring-Danes under the welkin and made safe by war many a tribe throughout the world with spears and swords, so that I recked not any man my foeman under the sweep of heaven. Lo! then there came to me change in my homeland, sorrow after gaming, when Grendel, that ancient foe became my invader. And ever I bore much sorrow of mind through that feud. And may God be thanked, the eternal lord, that I lingered in life, till I looked with mine eyes on that head stained with sword-blood after the old strife. Go now to thy seat and enjoy the feasting, thou who art glorious in war. And when morning cometh there shall be a host of treasures in common between us.'

And the Geat was glad of mind, and soon he went up to the high seat as the proud chief had bidden him. Then renewed was fair chanting as before 'mongst these brave ones who sat on the floor. And the helmet of night grew dark over men. And the noble warriors arose. The venerable king wished to go to his bed, the old prince of the Danes. And the Geat, the shield-warrior, desired greatly to go to his rest. And straightway a hall-thane guided the far-comer, weary of his journey, he who so carefully attended to all his needs such as that day the ocean-goers would fain be having. And the great-hearted one rested himself. The House towered on high that was spacious and gold-decked. The guest slept within until the black raven heralded the joy of heaven.

Then came the sun, hastening and shining over the earth. Warriors were hurrying and Athelings were eager to go to their people. The bold-hearted comer would visit the ship far away. He the hardy one bade the son of Ecglaf carry forth Hrunting, and commanded him to take his sword, that lovely piece of steel. And he gave thanks for the lending, and said he reckoned him a good war-comrade and crafty in fighting. Not at all did he blame the edge of the sword. He was a proud man. When ready for the journey were all the warriors, then Beowulf the Atheling, of good worth to the Danes, went up to the dais where was Hrothgar the faithful and bold, and greeted him there.

26

Beowulf spake, the son of Ecgtheow: 'Now we the sea-farers, that have come from afar, desire to say that we are hastening back to Hygelac. And here have we been nobly waited on, and well thou hast treated us. And if I then on earth can gain a whit further greater heart-love from thee, O Lord of men, than I have gained already, in doing war-deeds, thereto I'm right ready. And if I shall hear o'er the sheet of waters that terrors are oppressing those who sit round thee, as erewhile thine enemies were doing upon thee, I will bring here a thousand thanes, heroes to help thee. And I know that Hygelac, the Lord of the Geats, the guardian of my folk, though young in years, will help me by word and works to bring to thee honour and bear spear to thine aid, the help of strength, if thou hast need of men. And if Hrethric[42] the Prince's child should ever take service in the court of the Geat, he may find there many a friend. It is better for him who is doughty himself to be seeking far countries.'

Hrothgar spake and gave him answer: 'The all-knowing Lord doth send thee words into thy mind. Never heard I a man speak more wisely, so young in years, thou art strong of main and proud of soul, and of words a wise sayer. I reckon that if it cometh to pass that an arrow or fierce battle should take away the children of Hrethel or disease or sword destroy thy sovereign, the protector of the folk, and thou art still living, that the Sea-Geats will not have to choose any better king, if thou wilt hold the kingdom of the kinsmen. Thou hast brought about peace to the folk of the Geats and the Spear-Danes, and a ceasing of the strife and of the enmity which formerly they suffered. And whilst I am ruling the wide kingdom, treasures shall be in common between us. And many a man shall greet another with gifts over the sea.[43] And the ring-necked ship shall bear over the ocean both offerings and love-tokens. I know the two peoples to be steadfast towards friend and foe, and blameless in all things in the old wise.'

Then in that hall the prince of the earls, the son of Healfdene, gave him twelve treasures, and bade him be seeking his own people in safety and with the offerings, and quickly to come back again. Then the King, the Prince of the Danes, he of good lineage, kissed the best of thanes, and embraced his neck. And tears were falling down the face of the old man. And the old and wise man had hope of both things, but most of all of the other that they might see each the other, those thoughtful men in council.

For Beowulf was so dear to him that he could not restrain the whelming in his bosom, but a secret longing fast in the bonds of his soul was burning in his breast against his blood.[44] So Beowulf the warrior, proud of his golden gifts, went forth o'er the grassy plain rejoicing in treasure. And the sea-goer was awaiting her lord where she lay at anchor. And as he was going he often thought on the gift of Hrothgar. He was a king, blameless in every way, until old age, that scather of many, bereft him of the joys of strength.

27

So many a proud young warrior came to the seaside. And they were carrying the ring-net, the interlaced coats of mail. And the ward of the shore noticed the going of the earls, as he did their coming.[45] Nor with evil intent did he hail the guests from the edge of the cliff, but rode up to them, and said that welcome and bright-coated warriors went to the ship to the people of the Geats. Then on the sand was the spacious craft laden with battle-weeds, the ringed prow with horses and treasures, and the mast towered high over Hrothgar's gifts. And he gave to the captain a sword bound with gold, so that by the mead-bench he was by that the worthier because of the treasure and the heirloom. Then he went on board, the deep water to be troubling, and finally left the land of the Danes. And by the mast was one of the ocean-garments, a sail fast by a rope. The sea-wood thundered. Nor did the wind hinder the journey of that ship. The ocean-goer bounded forth, the foamy-necked one, over the waves, the bound prow over the ocean streams, till they could see the cliffs of the Geats' land, the well-known headlands.

Then the keel thronged up the shore, driven by the wind, and stood fast in the sand. And the harbour-master was soon on the seashore, who of yore eagerly had seen from afar the going forth of the dear men. And he made fast the wide-bosomed ship, by the anchor chains, so that the less the force of the waves could tear away that winsome ship. He commanded the treasure of the nobles to be borne up the beach, the fretted armour and the plated gold. And not far thence it was for them to be seeking the giver of treasure, Hygelac, Hrethel's son, for at home he dwelleth, he and his companions near to the sea-wall. And splendid was that building, and the Prince was a bold King, and the halls were high, and Hygd his wife was very young and wise and mature in her figure, though the daughter of Hæreth had bided in that city but a very few years. But she was not mean nor niggardly of gifts and of treasures to the people of the Geats.

But Thrytho[46] was fierce, for she had committed a terrible crime, that bold Queen of the folk. There was none that durst risk that dire thing of the dear companions, save only her lord, that he should stare on her with his eyes by day; but if he did he might expect that death-bands were destined for himself, for after the hand-grip a weapon was quickly prepared, that the sword that was curiously inlaid should bring to light and make known the death-bale. Nor is it a queenly custom for a woman to perform, though she might be peerless, that she should assail the life of a peace-wearer, of her dear lord, after a pretended insult. At least King Offa, the kinsman of Hemming, checked her in that. But otherwise said the ale-drinkers, namely that she did less of bale to her people and of hostile acts, since the time when she was first given all decked with gold to the young champion,[47] to her dear lord, since she sought the Hall of Offa over the fallow flood by the guidance of her father, where on the throne whilst she lived she well did enjoy her fate, that woman famous for good works. And she kept great love for the prince of heroes, and of all mankind he was, as I have learned by asking, the greatest by two seas. For Offa was a spear-keen man in gifts and in warfare, and widely was he honoured. And he ruled his people wisely. And to him and Thrytho Eomær was born to the help of heroes, he the kinsman of Hemming, the nephew of Garmund, was crafty in battle.

28

Then the hardy one himself, with his troop set forth to tread the sea-shore, going along the sands, the wide sea-beaches. The candle of the world shone, the sun that was shining from the South. And joyfully they journeyed, and with courage they marched along, to where they heard by inquiring, that the good Prince of earls, the banesman of Ongentheow[48] the young war-king, was giving out rings within the city. And quickly was made known to Hygelac the coming of Beowulf, that he the Prince of warriors, the comrade in arms, was returning alive and hale from the battle-play, was coming to the palace. And straightway was there room made for the foot-guests on the floor of the hall by command of the King. And he that had escaped scot-free from the contest sat with the King, kinsman with kinsman, and the lord with courteous speech saluted the brave man with high-swelling words. And the daughter of Hæreth[49] poured forth from the mead-cups throughout that great hall, for she loved well the people, and carried round the drinking-stoups to each of the warriors. And Hygelac began to question his comrade as curiosity prompted him as to the journey of the Sea-Geats. 'How went it with thee, dear Beowulf, in thy faring, when thou didst bethink thee suddenly to be seeking a contest o'er the salt waters, in battle at Hart? And thou didst requite the widely known woe which Hrothgar was suffering, that famous lord. And I brooded o'er that mind-care with sorrow-whelmings, for I trusted not in the journey of the dear man. And for a long time I bade thee not a whit to be greeting the murderous stranger, but to let the South Danes themselves wage war against Grendel. And I now give God thanks that I see thee safe and sound.'

Beowulf answered, the son of Ecgtheow: 'O Lord Hygelac, it is well known to many a man, our famous meeting, and the battle we fought, Grendel and I, on the wide plain, when he was working great sorrow to the Danes and misery for ever. All that I avenged, so that no kinsman of Grendel anywhere on earth needed to boast of that uproar by twilight, no not he of that kindred who liveth the longest, encircled by the fen. And first, to greet Hrothgar, I went to the Ring-hall. And straightway the famous kinsman of Healfdene, when he knew my intention, gave me a place with his own son; and the troop was all joyful. Nor ever have I seen greater joy amongst any hall-dwellers under the arch of heaven. Sometimes the famous Queen,[50] the peace-bringer of the folk, walked over the whole floor and encouraged the young sons. And often she gave to the man a twisted ring ere she went to the high seat. And sometimes for the noble band the daughter of Hrothgar carried the ale-cups to the earls at the end of the high table. And I heard those who sat in that hall calling her Freawaru as she gave the studded treasure to the heroes. And she, young and gold-decked, is betrothed to the glad son of Froda.[51] The friend of the Danes and the guardian of the kingdom has brought this to pass, and taken that counsel, so as to set at rest by that betrothal many a slaughter-feud and ancient strife. And often it happens that a little while after the fall of a people, the deadly spear seldom lieth at rest though the bride be doughty. And this may displease the lord of the Heathobards and all of his thanes of the people, when he with his bride walketh over the floor, that his doughty warriors should attend on a noble scion of the Danes, and the heirloom of the ancients should glisten on him, all hard, and the ring-sword, the treasure of the Heathobards, whilst they might be wielding weapons.[52]

29

'Till the day on which they risked their own and their comrades' lives in the battle. Then said an old spear-warrior who remembered all that had happened, the death of men by spears (his mind was grim), and he began with sorrowful mind to seek out the thought of the young champion by broodings of the heart, and to awaken the war-bales, and this is what he said: "Canst thou recognize, my friend, the dire sword which thy father carried to the battle, under the visored helm, on that last journey, when the Danes slew him and had the battle-field in their power, when Withergyld[54] lay dead after the fall of the heroes? Now here the son of I know not which of the slayers, all boasting of treasures, goeth into the hall and boasteth of murder and carrieth the gift which thou shouldst rightly possess." Then he exhorteth and bringeth to mind each of the occasions with sorrowful words, until the time cometh that the thane of the bride dieth all stained with blood for the deeds of his father by the piercing of the sword, having forfeited his life. But the other thence escapeth alive, for he knows the land well. Then the oath-swearing of earls is broken on both sides when deadly enmities surge up against Ingeld, and his love for his wife grows cooler after whelming care. And for this reason I reckon not sincere the friendliness of the Heathobards towards the Danes or the troop-peace between them, the plighted troth.

'Now I speak out again about Grendel, for that thou knowest full well, O giver of treasure, how went that hand-to-hand fight of the heroes. When the jewel of heaven glided over the world, then the angry sprite, the terrible and evening-fierce foe, came to visit us where we were dwelling in the hall all safe and sound. There was battle impending to Hondscio, the life-bale to the doomed one. And he first fell, the champion begirt. For Grendel was to the famous thane a banesman by biting, and devoured whole the dear man. Nor would he, the bloody-toothed slayer, mindful of bales, go out empty-handed any sooner again, forth from the gold-hall; but he proved my strength of main, and ready-handed he grasped at me. An ample and wondrous glove hung fast by cunning bands. And it was cunningly fashioned by the craft of devils, and with skins of the dragon. And the fierce doer of deeds was wishful to put me therein, one among many. But he could not do so, for I angrily stood upright. And too long would it be to tell how I requited all evil to that scather of the people, where I, O my liege-lord, honoured thy people by means of good deeds. He escaped on the way, and for a little while he enjoyed life-pleasures. But his right hand showed his tracks in Hart, and he sank to the bottom of the sea, all abject and sad of heart. And the lord of the Danes rewarded me for that battle-rush with many a piece of plated gold, and with ample treasure, when morning came and we had set ourselves down to the feasting. And there was singing and rejoicing. And the wise man of the Danes, who had learned many things, told us of olden days. And the bold in battle sometimes touched the harp-strings, the wood that was full of music, and sometimes he gave forth a song that was true and sad—and sometimes, large-hearted, the King related a wondrous spell well and truly.[55] And sometimes the old man encumbered by years, some ancient warrior, lamented his lost youth and strength in battle. His heart was tumultuous when he, of many winters, recalled all the number of them. So we rejoiced the livelong day until another night came down upon men. Then was the mother of Grendel quickly ready for vengeance, and came on a woful journey, for Death had carried off her son, that war-hate of the Geats. And the uncanny wife avenged her child. And Aeschere, that wise and ancient councillor, departed this life. Nor when morning came might the Danish people burn him with brand, that death-weary man, nor lay the beloved man on the funeral pyre. For she bore away the body in her fiendish grip under the mountain-streams. And that was to Hrothgar the bitterest of griefs which for long had befallen the Prince of the people. Then the Prince, sad in mood, by thy life entreated me that I should do a deed, worthy of an earl, midst welter of waters, and risk my life and achieve glory. And he promised me rewards. I then discovered the grim and terrible guardian of the whelming waters, at the sea's bottom, so widely talked of. There was a hand-to-hand engagement between us for a while, and the sea boiled with gore; I cut off the head of Grendel's mother in the hall at the bottom of the sea, with powerful sword. And I scarce saved my life in that conflict. But not yet was my doomsday. And afterwards the Prince of earls gave me many gifts, he the son of Healfdene.

31

'So in good customs lived the King of the people. Nor had I lost the rewards, the meed of strength, for the son of Healfdene bestowed upon me treasures according to my choice, which I will bring to thee, O my warrior-King, and graciously will I proffer them. Again all favour depends on thee, for few chief kinsmen have I save thee, O Hygelac.' He commanded them to bring in the boar, the head-sign, the battle-steep helmet, the hoary byrny, the splendid war-sword, and then he chanted this song: 'It was Hrothgar, that proud prince, who bestowed upon me all this battle-gear. And a certain word he uttered to me, that I should first give thee his kindly greeting.[56] He said that Hrothgar the King of the Danes possessed it a long while. Nor formerly would he be giving the breast-weeds to his son the brave Heoroward, though dear he was to him. Do thou enjoy all well.'

Then I heard that four horses, of reddish yellow hue, followed the armour. And thus he did him honour with horses and gifts. So should a kinsman do. By no means should they weave cunning nets for each other, or with secret craft devise death to a comrade. His nephew was very gracious to Hygelac, the brave in strife, and each was striving to bestow favours on the other. And I heard that he gave to Hygd the neck-ring so curiously and wondrously wrought, which Wealtheow a daughter of royal birth had given him, and three horses also slender and saddle-bright. And her breast was adorned with the ring she had received.

And Beowulf, son of Ecgtheow, so famous in warfare and in good deeds, bore himself boldly and fulfilled his fate, nor did he slay the drunken hearth-comrades. He was not sad-minded, but he, the battle-dear one, by the greatest of craft known to man held fast the lasting and generous gift which God gave him. For long had he been despised, so that the warriors of the Geats looked not upon him as a good man, nor did the lord of troops esteem him as of much worth on the mead-bench. Besides, they thought him slack and by no means a warlike Atheling. Then came a change from all his distresses to this glorious man. Then the Prince of Earls, the battle-brave King, commanded that the heirloom of Hrethel all decked out in gold should be brought in. For of swords there was no more glorious treasure among the Geats. And he laid it on the bosom of Beowulf, and gave him seven thousand men and a building and a throne. And both of them held the land, the earth, the rights in the land as an hereditary possession; but the other who was the better man had more especially a wide kingdom.

And in after-days it happened that there were battle-crashings, and Hygelac lay dead,[57] and swords under shields became a death-bane to Heardred,[58] when the brave battle-wolves, the Swedes, sought him out among the victorious ones and assailed with strife the nephew of Hereric, and it was then that the broad kingdom came into the possession of Beowulf. And he held sway therein fifty winters (and a wise King was he, that old guardian of his country) until on dark nights a dragon began to make raids, he that watched over the hoard in the lofty cavern, the steep rocky cave. And the path thereto lay under the cliffs unknown to men. And what man it was who went therein I know not, but he took from the heathen hoard a hall-bowl decked with treasure. Nor did he give it back again, though he had beguiled the guardian of the hoard when he was sleeping, by the craft of a thief. And Beowulf found out that the dragon was angry.[59]

32

And it was by no means of his own accord or self-will that he sought out the craft of the hoard of the dragon who inflicted such evil upon himself, but rather because being compelled by miseries, the slave fled the hateful blows of heroes, he that was shelterless and the man troubled by guilt penetrated therein. And soon it came to pass that an awful terror arose upon the guest.[60] . . . And in the earth-house were all kinds of ancient treasures, such as I know not what man of great thoughts had hidden there in days of old, the immense heirlooms of some noble race, costly treasures. And in former times death had taken them all away, and he alone of the warriors of the people who longest lingered there, full lonely and sad for loss of friends was he, and he hoped for a tarrying, that he but for a little while might enjoy the ancient treasures. And this hill was quite near to the ocean-waves, and to the sea-nesses, and no one could come near thereto.

And he the guardian of rings carried inside the cave the heavy treasures of plated gold, and uttered some few words: 'Do thou, O earth, hold fast the treasures of earls which heroes may not hold. What! From thee in days of yore good men obtained it. Deadly warfare and terrible life-bale carried away all the men of my people of those who gave up life. They had seen hall-joy. And they saw the joys of heaven. I have not any one who can carry a sword or polish the gold-plated cup, the dear drinking-flagon. The doughty ones have hastened elsewhere. The hard helmet dight with gold shall be deprived of gold plate. The polishers sleep the sleep of death who should make ready the battle grim, likewise the coat of mail which endured in the battle was shattered over shields by the bite of the iron spears and perishes after the death of the warrior. Nor can the ringed byrny go far and wide on behalf of heroes, after the passing of the war-chief.

'No joy of harping is there, nor mirth of stringed instruments, nor does the goodly hawk swing through the hall, nor doth the swift horse paw in the courtyard. And death-bale hath sent away many generations of men.' Thus then, sad at heart he lamented his sorrowful plight, one for many, and unblithely he wept both day and night until the whelming waters of death touched his heart. And the ancient twilight scather found the joyous treasure standing open and unprotected, he it was who flaming seeks the cliff-sides, he, the naked and hateful dragon who flieth by night wrapt about with fire. And the dwellers upon earth greatly fear him. And he should be seeking the hoard upon earth where old in winters he guardeth the heathen gold. Nor aught is he the better thereby.

And thus the scather of the people, the mighty monster, had in his power the hall of the hoard three hundred years upon the earth until a man in anger kindled his fury. For he carried off to his liege-lord the plated drinking-flagon and offered his master a treaty of peace. Thus was the hoard discovered, the hoard of rings plundered. And a boon was granted to the miserable man. And the Lord saw for the first time this ancient work of men. Then awoke the dragon, and the strife was renewed. He sniffed at the stone, and the stout-hearted saw the foot-mark of his foe. He had stepped too far forth with cunning craft near the head of the dragon. So may any one who is undoomed easily escape woes and exile who rejoices in the favour of the Wielder of the world. The guardian of the hoard, along the ground, was eagerly seeking, and the man would be finding who had deprived him of his treasure while he was sleeping. Hotly and fiercely he went around all on the outside of the barrow—but no man was there in the waste. Still he gloried in the strife and the battle working. Sometimes he returned to the cavern and sought the treasure vessels. And soon he found that one of the men had searched out the gold, the high heap of treasures. The guardian of the hoard was sorrowfully waiting until evening should come. And very furious was the keeper of that barrow, and the loathsome one would fain be requiting the robbery of that dear drinking-stoup with fire and flame. Then, as the dragon wished, day was departing. Not any longer would he wait within walls, but went forth girt with baleful fire. And terrible was this beginning to the people in that country, and sorrowful would be the ending to their Lord, the giver of treasure.

33

Then the Fiend began to belch forth fire, and to burn up the glorious palace. And the flames thereof were a horror to men. Nor would the loathly air-flier leave aught living thereabouts. And this warfare of the dragon was seen far and wide by men, this striving of the foe who caused dire distress, and how the war-scather hated and harmed the people of the Geats. And he hurried back to his hoard and the dark cave-hall of which he was lord, ere it was day-dawn. He had encircled the dwellers in that land with fire and brand. He trusted in his cavern, and in battle and his cliff-wall. But his hope deceived him. Then was the terror made known to Beowulf, quickly and soothly, namely that his very homestead, that best of houses, that throne of the Geats, was dissolving in the whelming fire. And full rueful was it to the good man, and the very greatest of sorrows.

And the wise man was thinking that he had bitterly angered the Wielder of all things, the eternal God, in the matter of some ancient customs.[61] And within his breast gloomy brooding was welling, as was by no means his wont. The fiery dragon had destroyed by flame the stronghold of the people, both the sea-board and neighbouring land. And therefore the King of the Weder-Geats devised revenge upon him.

Now Beowulf the Prince of earls and protector of warriors commanded them to fashion him a glorious war-shield all made of iron. For he well knew that a wooden shield would be unavailing against flames. For he, the age-long noble Atheling, must await the end of days that were fleeting of this world-life, he and the dragon together, though long he had held sway over the hoard of treasure. And the Prince of rings scorned to employ a troop against the wide-flying monster in the great warfare. Nor did he dread the striving, nor did he think much of this battle with the dragon, of his might and courage, for that formerly in close conflict had he escaped many a time from the crashings of battle since he, the victorious sword-man, cleansed the great hall in Hart, of Hrothgar his kinsman, and had grappled in the contest with the mother of Grendel, of the loathly kin.

Nor was that the least hand-to-hand fight, when Hygelac was slain there in the Frisian land when the King of the Geats, the friendly lord of the folk, the son of Hrethel, died in the battle-rush beaten down by the sword, drunk with blood-drinking. Then fled Beowulf by his very own craft and swam through the seas.[62] And he had on his arm alone thirty battle-trappings when he went down to the sea. Nor did the Hetware need to be boasting, of that battle on foot, they who bore their linden shields against him. And few of them ever reached their homes safe from that wolf of the battle.

But Beowulf, son of Ecgtheow, swam o'er the expanse of waters, miserable and solitary, back to his people, where Hygd proffered him treasures and a kingdom, rings and dominion. She did not think that her son Heardred would know how to hold their native seats against strangers, now that Hygelac was dead. Nor could the wretched people prevail upon the Atheling (Beowulf) in any wise to show himself lord of Heardred or to be choosing the kingship. Nevertheless he gave friendly counsel to the folk with grace and honour until that he (Heardred) was older and held sway over the Weder-Geats.

Then those exiles the sons of Ohthere sought him over the seas; they had rebelled against the Lord of the Swedes, the best of the sea-kings, that famous chieftain of those who bestowed rings in Sweden. And that was life's limit to him. For the son of Hygelac, famishing there, was allotted a deadly wound by the swing of a sword. And the son of Ongentheow went away thence to visit his homestead when Heardred lay dead, and left Beowulf to sit on the throne and to rule the Goths. And he was a good King.[63]

34

He was minded in after-days to be requiting the fall of the prince. He was a friend to the wretched Eadgils, and helped Eadgils the son of Ohthere with an army with warriors and with weapons, over the wide seas. And then he wrought vengeance with cold and painful journeyings and deprived the king (Onela) of life.[64] Thus the son of Ecgtheow had escaped all the malice and the hurtful contests and the courageous encounters, until the day on which he was to wage war with the dragon. And so it came to pass that the Lord of the Geats went forth with twelve others and inflamed with fury, to spy out the dragon. For he had heard tell of the malice and hatred he had shown to men, whence arose that feud.

And by the hand of the informer,[65] famous treasure came into their possession; he was the thirteenth man in the troop who set on foot the beginning of the conflict. And the sorrowful captive must show the way thither. He against his will went to the earth-hall, for he alone knew the barrow under the ground near to the sea-surge, where it was seething, the cavern that was full of ornaments and filagree. And the uncanny guardian thereof, the panting war-wolf, held possession of the treasures, and an ancient was he under the earth. And it was no easy bargain to be gaining for any living man.

So the battle-hardened King sat down on the cliff, and took leave of his hearth-comrades, he the gold-friend of the Geats. And his heart was sad, wavering, and ready for death, and Weird came very near to him who would be greeting the venerable warrior and be seeking his soul-treasure, to divide asunder his life from his body. And not long after that was the soul of the Atheling imprisoned in the flesh. Beowulf spake, the son of Ecgtheow: 'Many a war-rush I escaped from in my youth, in times of conflict. And well I call it all to mind. I was seven years old when the Lord of Treasures, the friendly lord of the folk, took me away from my father—and King Hrethel had me in thrall, and gave me treasure and feasted me and kept the peace. Nor was I a whit less dear a child to him than any of his own kin, Herebald and Hæthcyn or my own dear Hygelac. And for the eldest was a murder-bed most unhappily made up by the deeds of a kinsman,[66] when Hæthcyn his lordly friend brought him low with an arrow from out of his horn-bow, and missing the mark he shot through his brother with a bloody javelin. And that was a fight not to be atoned for by gifts of money; and a crime it was, and wearying to the soul in his breast. Nevertheless the Atheling must unavenged be losing his life. For so is it a sorrowful thing for a venerable man to see his son riding the gallows-tree when he singeth a dirge a sorrowful song, as his son hangeth, a joy to the ravens. And he, very old, may not give him any help. And every morning at the feasting he is reminded of his son's journey else-whither. And he careth not to await another heir within the cities, when he alone through the fatality of death hath found out the deeds.

'Heartbroken he looks on the bower of his son, on the wasted wine-hall, become the hiding-place for the winds and bereft of the revels. The riders are sleeping, the heroes in the tomb. Nor is any sound of harping, or games in the courts as erewhile there were.

35

'Then he goeth to the sleeping-place and chanteth a sorrow-song, the one for the other. And all too spacious seemed to him the fields and the dwelling-house. So the Prince of the Geats bore welling heart-sorrow after Herebald's death, nor a whit could he requite the feud on the murderer, nor visit his hate on that warrior with loathly deeds, though by no means was he dear to him. He then forsook the joys of life because of that sorrow-wound which befell him, and chose the light of God, and left to his sons land and towns when he departed this life as a rich man doth. Then was there strife and struggle between the Swedes and the Geats, and over the wide seas there was warfare between them, a hardy battle-striving when Hrethel met with his death. And the children of Ongentheow were brave and battle-fierce, and would not keep the peace on the high seas, but round about Hreosnaborg they often worked terrible and dire distress. And my kinsmen wrought vengeance for that feud and crime as all men know, though the other bought his life with a hard bargain. And war was threatening Hæthcyn the lord of the Geats. Then I heard tell that on the morrow one brother the other avenged on the slayer with the edge of the sword, whereas Ongentheow[67] seeketh out Eofor. The war-helmet was shattered, and the Ancient of the Swedes fell prone, all sword-pale. And well enough the hand kept in mind the feud and withheld not the deadly blow. And I yielded him back in the warfare the treasures he gave me with the flashing sword, as was granted to me. And he gave me land and a dwelling and a pleasant country. And he had no need to seek among the Gifthas or the Spear-Danes or in Sweden a worse war-wolf, or to buy one that was worthy.

'And I would always be before him in the troop, alone in the front of the battle, and so for ever will I be striving, whilst this sword endureth, that earlier and later has often stood me in good stead, since the days when for doughtiness I was a hand-slayer to Day Raven the champion of the Hugs. Nor was he fated to bring ornaments or breast-trappings to the Frisian King, but he the guardian of the standard, he the Atheling, fell on the battle-field, all too quickly. Nor was the sword-edge his bane, but the battle-grip broke the whelmings of his heart and the bones of his body. Now shall my sword-edge, my hand and hard weapon, be fighting for the hoard.'

Beowulf moreover now for the last time spake these boastful words: 'In many a war I risked my life in the days of my youth, yet still will I seek a feud, I the old guardian of the people will work a glorious deed if the wicked scather cometh out from his earth-palace to seek me.'

Then he saluted for the last time each of the warriors, the brave wearers of helmets, the dear companions. 'I would not carry a sword or weapon against the dragon if I knew how else I might maintain my boast against the monster, as I formerly did against Grendel. But in this conflict I expect the hot battle-fire, both breath and poison. Therefore I have both shield and byrny. I will not flee from the warder of the barrow a foot's-space, but it shall be with me at the wall of the barrow as Weird shall direct, who created all men. I am strong in soul so that I will refrain from boasting against the war-flier. Await ye on the barrow guarded by byrnies, O ye warriors in armour, and see which of us two will better survive his wounds after the battle-rush. This is no journey for you nor fitting for any man save only for me, that he should share a conflict with the monster and do deeds worthy of an earl. I will gain possession of the gold by my courage, or battle and deadly evil shall take away your lord.'

Then the strong warrior, hard under helm, arose beside his shield and carried his shirt of mail under the rocky cliffs and trusted in the strength of himself alone. Nor was that a coward's journey. Then Beowulf, possessed of manly virtues, who had escaped in many a conflict and crashing of battle when men encountered on foot, saw standing by the wall of the barrow an arch of rock, and a stream broke out thence from the barrow, and the whelming of that river was hot with battle-fires. Nor could he survive any while near to the hoard unburnt because of the flame of the dragon. Then in a fury the Prince of the Weder-Geats let a torrent of words escape from his breast and the stout-hearted one stormed. And his war-clear voice resounded under the hoar cliffs. And hatred was stirred, for the guardian of the hoard recognized well the voice of Beowulf. And that was no time to be seeking friendship. And the breath of the monster, the hot battle-sweat, came forth from the rock at the first and the earth resounded. The warrior, the Lord of the Geats, raised his shield under the barrow against the terrible sprite. Now the heart of the dragon was stirred up to seek the conflict. The good war-king had formerly drawn his sword, the ancient heirloom, not slow of edge. And each of them who intended evil was a terror the one to the other. And the stern-minded one, he the Prince of friendly rulers, stood by his steep shield, and he and the dragon fell quickly together. Beowulf waited warily all in his war-gear. Then the flaming monster bent as he charged, hastening to his doom. The shield well protected life and body of the famous warrior for a lesser while than he had willed it if he was to be wielding victory in that contest on the first day; but Weird had not so fated it. And the Lord of the Geats uplifted his hand, and struck at the horribly bright one heavy with heirlooms, so that the edge stained with blood gave way on the bone and bit in less strongly than its master had need of when pressed by the business. Then after the battle-swing the guardian of the barrow was rough-minded and cast forth slaughter-fire. Battle-flames flashed far and wide. And the son of the Geats could not boast of victory in the conflict. The sword had failed him, naked in the battle, as was unfitting for so well tempered a steel. And it was not easy for the famous son of Ecgtheow to give up possession of the bottom of the sea, and that he should against his will dwell in some place far otherwhere, as must each man let go these fleeting days sooner or later. And not long after this Beowulf and the monster met together again. The guardian of the hoard took good heart, and smoke was fuming in his breast. And fierce were his sufferings as the flames embraced him, he who before had ruled over the folk. Nor at all in a troop did his hand-comrades stand round him, that warrior of Athelings, showing courage in the battle, but they fled into a wood their lives to be saving. And the mind of one of them was surging with sorrows, for to him whose thoughts are pure, friendship cannot ever change.

36

Wiglaf was he called, he who was the son of Weohstan, the beloved
shield-warrior, the Prince of the Danes and the kinsman of Aelfhere.
He saw his lord suffering burning pain under his visor. Then he
called to mind the favour that he (Beowulf) had bestowed upon him
in days of yore, the costly dwelling of the Waegmundings[68] and all the
folk-rights which his father had possessed. Then he could not restrain
himself, but gripped the shield with his hand, the yellow wood, and
drew forth the old sword which was known among men as the heirloom
of Eanmund, the son of Ohthere, and in the striving Weohstan was
banesman by the edge of the sword to that friendless exile and bore
away to his kinsman the brown-hued helmet, the ringed byrny, and
the old giant's sword that Onela[69] had given him, the war-weeds of his
comrade, and the well-wrought armour for fighting. Nor did he speak
of the feud, though he slew his brother's son. And he held possession
of the treasures many years, both the sword and the byrny, until such
time as his son should hold the earlship as his father had done. And
he gave to the Geats a countless number of each kind of war-weeds,
when he in old age passed away from this life, on the outward journey.
That was the first time for the young champion that he went into the
war-rush with his noble lord. Nor did his mind melt within him, nor
did the heirloom of his kinsman at the war-tide. And the dragon discovered it when they two came together.

Wiglaf spake many fitting words, and said to his comrades (for his
mind was sad within him): 'I remember the time when we partook of
the mead, and promised our liege-lord in the beer-hall, he who gave to
us rings, that we would yield to him war-trappings both helmets and a
hand-sword, if such need befell him. And he chose us for this warfare,
and for this journey, of his own free will, and reminded us of glory; and
to me he gave these gifts when he counted us good spear-warriors and
brave helmet-bearers, although our lord, this guardian of the people
had it in his mind all alone to do this brave work for us, for he most
of all men could do glorious things and desperate deeds of war. And
now is the day come that our lord hath need of our prowess and of

goodly warriors. Let us then go to the help of our battle-lord while it lasts, the grim terror of fire. God knows well of me that I would much rather that the flame should embrace my body together with that of my lord the giver of gold. Nor does it seem to me to be fitting that we should carry shields back to the homestead except we have first laid low the foe and protected the life of the Prince of the Weders.[70] And well I know that his old deserts were not that he alone of the youth of the Geats should suffer grief and sink in the fighting. So both sword and helmet, byrny and shield shall be common to both of us together.'

Then he waded through the slaughter-reek, and bore the war-helmet to the help of his lord, and uttered a few words: 'Beloved Beowulf, do thou be doing all things, as thou of yore in the days of thy youth wast saying that thou wouldst not allow thy glory to be dimmed whilst thou wast living. Now shalt thou, the brave in deeds and the resolute noble, save thy life with all thy might. I am come to help thee.' After these words came the angry dragon, the terrible and hostile sprite yet once again, and decked in his various hues of whelmings of fire, against his enemies, the men that he hated. And the wood of the shield was burnt up with the waves of flame, and his byrny could not help the young spear-warrior; yet did the youth bravely advance under the shield of his kinsman when his own had been destroyed by the flames. Then again the war-king bethought him of glory, and struck a mighty blow with his battle-sword so that it fixed itself in his head, forced in by violence. And Naegling, Beowulf's sword old and grey, broke in pieces, and failed in the contest. It was not given to him that sharp edges of swords should help him in battle. His hand was too strong, so that it overtaxed every sword, as I have been told, by the force of its swing, whenever he carried into battle a wondrous hand-weapon. And he was nowise the better for a sword. Then for the third time, the scather of the people, the terrible Fire-dragon, was mindful of feuds, and he rushed on the brave man when he saw that he had room, all hot and battle-grim, and surrounded his neck with bitter bones. And he was all be-bloodied over with life-blood, and the sweat welled up in waves.

37

Then I heard tell that the Earl of the King of the People showed in his
time of need unfailing courage in helping him with craft and keenness,
as was fitting for him to do. He paid no heed to the head of the dragon
(but the brave man's hand was being burnt when he helped his kinsman), but that warrior in arms struck at the hostile sprite somewhat
lower in his body so that his shining and gold-plated sword sank into
his body, and the fire proceeding therefrom began to abate. Then the
good King Beowulf got possession of his wits again, and drew his bitter
and battle-sharp short sword that he bore on his shield. And the King
of the Geats cut asunder the dragon in the midst of his body. And the
fiend fell prone; courage had driven out his life, and they two together
had killed him, noble comrades in arms. And thus should a man who
is a thane always be helping his lord at his need. And that was the very
last victory achieved by that Prince during his life-work.

Then the wound which the Earth-dragon had formerly dealt him
began to burn and to swell. And he soon discovered that the baleful
venom was seething in his breast, the internal poison. Then the young
noble looked on the giant's work as he sat on a seat musing by the cliff
wall, how arches of rock, firmly on columns held the eternal earth-
house within. Then the most noble thane refreshed his blood-stained
and famous Lord, his dear and friendly Prince with water, with his
own hands, and loosened the helmet for the battle-sated warrior. And
Beowulf spake, over his deathly pitiful wound, for well he knew that
he had enjoyed the day's while of his earthly joy: and the number of
his days was all departed and death was coming very near.

'Now,' said Beowulf, 'I would have given battle-weeds to my son if any
heir had been given to me of my body. I held sway over these peoples
fifty years. And there was no folk-king of those who sat round about
who dared to greet me with swords, or oppress with terror. At home
have I bided my appointed time, and well I held my own[71], nor did I
seek out cunning feuds, nor did I swear many unrighteous oaths. And
I, sick of my life-wounds, can have joy of all this. For the Wielder of
men cannot reproach me with murder of kinsmen when my life shall

pass forth from my body. Now do thou, beloved Wiglaf, go quickly and look on the hoard under the hoar stone, now that the dragon lieth prone and asleep sorely wounded and bereft of his treasure. And do thou make good speed that I may look upon the ancient gold treasures and yarely be feasting mine eyes upon the bright and cunning jewels, so that thereby after gazing on that wealth of treasure I may the more easily give up my life and my lordship over the people, whom I have ruled so long.'

38

Then straightway I heard tell how the son of Weohstan, after these words had been spoken, obeyed the behest of his lord, who was sick of his wounds, and carried the ring-net and the coat of mail adorned, under the roof of the barrow. And as Wiglaf, exulting in victory, came by the seat, he saw many gems shining and shaped like the sun[72] and gleaming gold all lying on the ground, and wondrous decorations on the wall, and he saw too the den of the dragon, the ancient twilight-flier, and flagons standing there and vessels of men of days long gone by, no longer polished but shorn of adornment. And there also was many a helmet, ancient and rusty, and many arm-rings cunningly twisted.

The possession of treasure and of gold on the earth may easily make proud all of mankind, let him hide it who will. Likewise he saw the all-gilded banner lying high over the hoard, that greatest of wondrous handiwork and all woven by the skill of human hands. And therefrom went forth a ray of light, so that he could see the floor of the cave, and look carefully at the jewels. And there was no sign of the dragon, for the sword-edge had carried him off.

Then I heard tell how in that barrow one at his own doom[73] plundered the hoard, that old work of giants, and bore away on his arms both cups and dishes. And the banner also he took, that brightest of beacons. Beowulf's sword, with its iron edge, had formerly injured him who had been the protector of these treasures for a long time, and had waged fierce flame-terror, because of the hoard fiercely welling in the midnight hour until he was killed.

The messenger[74] was in haste, and eager for the return journey, and laden with jewels, and curiosity tormented him as to whether he would find the bold-minded Prince of the Geats alive on the battle-field, and bereft of strength where before he had left him. Then he with the treasures found the glorious lord, his own dear master, at the last gasp, and all stained with blood. And he began to throw water upon him, until the power of speech brake through his mind, and Beowulf spake, and with sorrow he looked upon the hoard.

'I would utter words of thanks to the Lord and wondrous King, to the eternal God, for the treasures which now I am looking upon that I have managed to obtain them for my dear people before my death-day. Now that I have in exchange for this hoard of treasure sold my life in my old age, and laid it down, do thou still be helping the people in their need, for I may no longer be lingering here. Do thou bid the famous warriors erect a burial-mound, after the burning of the funeral pyre, at the edge of the sea, which shall tower aloft on Whale's Ness, as a memorial for my people, and so the sea-farers shall call it the Hill of Beowulf, even those who drive the high ships from afar through the mists of the flood.'

Then he the bold Prince doffed from his neck the golden ring. And he gave it to his thane, to the young spear-warrior, the gold-adorned helmet, the ring, and the byrny, and bade him enjoy it well. 'Thou, O Wiglaf,' he said, 'art the last heir of our race, of that of the Waegmundings. Weird has swept away all my kinsmen to their fated doom, all the earls in their strength, and I shall follow after them.'

Now that was the very last word of the old warrior's breast thoughts, ere he chose the funeral pyre the hot wave-whelmings. And his soul went forth from his breast to be seeking the doom of the truth-fast ones.

39

Then had it sorrowfully come to pass for the young warrior that he saw his most beloved in a miserable plight on the earth at his life's end. Likewise the terrible dragon, his slayer, lay there bereft of life and pressed sore by ruin. And the coiled dragon could no longer wield the hoard of rings, but the iron edges of the sword, well tempered and battle-gashed; the hammer's leavings[75], had carried him off, so that the wide-flier, stilled because of his wounds, fell to the earth near to the hoard-hall. And no more in playful wise at the midnight hour, did he drift through the air; this dragon, proud in his gainings of treasure, showed not his face, but was fallen to the earth because of the handiwork of the battle-warrior.

And as I have heard, it would have profited but few of the mighty men, even though they were doughty in deeds of all kinds, though they should rush forth against the flaming breath of the poisonous scather, even to the very disturbing of the Ring-Hall with their hands, if they should have found the guardian thereof awake, and dwelling in the cliff-cave. Then Beowulf's share of lordly treasure was paid for by his death. And both he and the dragon had come to an end of their fleeting days.

And not long after that, the laggards in battle, those cowardly treaty-breakers, ten of them together, came back from the woodlands, they who erewhile had dreaded the play of javelins when their lord had sore need of their help. But they were filled with shame, and carried their shields, and battle-weeds, to where the old prince was lying. And they looked on Wiglaf; he the foot-warrior sat aweary near to the shoulders of his lord, and sought to rouse him by sprinkling water upon him, but he succeeded not at all. Nor could he, though he wished it ever so much, keep life in the chieftain or avert a whit the will of the Wielder of all things. Every man's fate was decided by the act of God, as is still the case. Then was a grim answer easily given by the young man to these who erewhile had lost their courage.

Wiglaf spake, he the son of Weohstan, the sad-hearted. 'He who will speak truth may say that the lord and master who gave you gifts, and warlike trappings, in which ye are now standing, when he very often gave on the ale-bench to them who sat in the hall, both helmet and byrny, the Prince to his thanes, as he could find any of you most noble far or near, that he wholly wrongly bestowed upon you war-trappings when war befell him. The King of the folk needed not indeed to boast of his army comrades, yet God, the Wielder of Victory, granted to him that alone he avenged himself with the edge of the sword when he had need of strength. And but a little life-protection could I give him in the battle, yet I sought to help him beyond my strength. The dragon was by so much the weaker when I struck with my sword that deadly foe. And less fiercely the fire surged forth from his head. Too few were the defenders thronged around their lord when his fated hour came. And now shall the receiving of treasure, and the gift of swords, and all joy of home and hope cease for ever to men of your kin. And every man of you of the tribe must wander empty of land-rights, since noble men will learn far and wide of your flight and inglorious deed. Death would be better for earls than a life of reproach.'

40

Then he bade them announce that battle-work at the entrenchment up over the sea-cliff where that troop of earls sat sorrowful in soul through the morning-long day, holding their shields and in expectation of the end of the day and the return of the dear man. And he who rode to and fro o'er the headland was little sparing of fresh tidings, but said to all who were sitting there, 'Now is the joy-giver of the people of the Geats fast on his death-bed, and by the deed of the dragon he inhabits the place of rest gained by a violent death. And by his side lieth the enemy of his life, sick of his dagger-wounds. Nor could he inflict with the sword any wound on that monster. Wiglaf sits over Beowulf, he the son of Weohstan, the earl over the other one who is dead, and reverently keeps ward over the loathèd and the belovèd. But there is an expectation of a time of war to the people, since to Franks and Frisians the fall of the King has become widely known. The hard strife was shapen against the Hugs, when Hygelac came with a fleet into the Frisian lands[76] where the Hetware overcame him in battle, and by their great strength and courage brought it to pass that the shield-warrior should stoop. He fell in the troop. Nor did the Prince give jewelled armour to the doughty ones. The mercy of the Merewing[77] was not always shown to us. Nor do I expect aught of peace or good faith from the Swedish People. But it was well known that Ongentheow[78] bereft Hæthcyn the son of Hrethel[79] of life over against Ravenswood, when because of pride the warlike Swedes first sought out the people of the Geats. Soon Ongentheow the wise father of Ohthere, the ancient and terrible, gave him (Hæthcyn) a return blow, destroyed the sea-kings, and rescued his bride (Queen Elan) he the old man rescued his wife bereft of gold, the mother of Onela and of Ohthere, and then followed up the deadly foe until with difficulty they retreated all lord-less to Ravenswood. And he attacked the remnant[80] with a great army, weary though he was with his wounds. And the live-long night he vowed woe upon the wretched troop, and said that on the morrow he would by the edge of the sword slay some and hang them up on the gallows-tree for a sport of the birds. But help came to the sorrowful in soul at the dawn of day, when they heard the horn of Hygelac and the blast of his trumpet when the good man came on the track faring with the doughty warriors of the people.

41

'And the blood-track of both Swedes and Geats, the slaughter-rush of warriors, was widely seen how the folk stirred up the feud amongst them. The good man, wise and very sad, went away with his comrades to seek out a stronghold. Earl Ongentheow turned away to higher ground, for he the war-crafty one had heard of the prowess of Hygelac the proud. He had no trust in his power to resist, or that he would be able to refuse the demands of the seamen, the ocean-farers, or defend the treasure he had taken, the children and the bride.[81] Thence afterwards, being old, he sought refuge under the earth-wall. Then was chase given to the people of the Swedes and the banner of Hygelac borne aloft; and they swept o'er the field of peace when the sons of Hrethel thronged to the entrenchment. And there too, was Ongentheow, he the grey-haired King of the People driven to bay at the edge of the sword, and forced to submit to the sole doom of Eofor. And angrily did Wulf, son of Wanred, smite him with weapon, so that from that swinging blow blood-sweat gushed forth in streams under the hair of his head. Yet the old Swede was not terrified thereby, but quickly gave back a terrible blow by a worse exchange when the King of the people turned thither. Nor could Wulf the bold son of Wanred give back a blow to the old churl, for Ongentheow had formerly cut his helmet in two, so that he, stained with blood, fell prone perforce to the ground. But not yet was he doomed, but he raised himself up, though the wound touched him close. And the hardy thane of Hygelac (Eofor) when his brother lay prostrate, caused the broad sword, the old giant's sword, to crash through the wall of shields upon the gigantic helmet. Then stooped the King, the shepherd of the people, mortally wounded. And there were many who bound up his kinsman and quickly upraised him when room had been made so that they might possess the battle-field, while one warrior was plundering another. One took the iron shield of Ongentheow, and his hard-hilted sword, and his helmet, and carried the trappings of the old man to Hygelac. And he received the treasures, and fairly he promised reward for the people, and he did as he promised. The lord of the Geats (Hygelac) son of Hrethel, rewarded with very costly gifts the battle onset of Eofor and Wulf when he got back to his palace, and bestowed upon each of them a hundred thousand, of land and locked rings. Nor could any man in the world reproach him for that reward, since they had gained glory by fighting; and he gave to Eofor his only daughter, she who graced his homestead, to wed as a favour. And this is the feud and the enmity and hostile strife of men, which I expect the Swedish people will seek to awaken against us when they shall hear we have lost our Prince, he who in days of yore held treasure and kingdom against our foes after the fall of heroes, and held in check the fierce Swedes, and did what was good for the people and deeds worthy of an earl. Now is it best for us to hasten to look upon our King and bring him who gave to us rings to the funeral pyre. Nor shall a part only of the treasure be melted with the proud man, but there is a hoard of wealth, an immense mass of gold, bought at a grim cost, for now at the very end of his life he bought for us rings. And the brands shall devour all the treasures and the flames of the funeral fire, they shall enfold them, nor shall an earl carry away any treasure as a memorial, nor shall any maid all beauteous wear on her neck ring adornments, but shall go sad of soul and bereft of gold, and often not once only tread an alien land now that the battle-wise man (Beowulf) has laid aside laughter, the games and the joys of song. And many a morning cold shall the spear in the hand-grip be heaved up on high, nor shall there be the sound of harping to awaken the warriors, but the war-raven, eager over the doomed ones, shall say many things to the eagle how it fared with him in eating the carrion while he, with the wolf, plundered the slaughtered.'

Thus then was the brave warrior reciting loathly spells. And he lied not at all in weird or word. Then the troop rose up together, and all unblithely went under Eagles' Ness, to look on the wonder, and tears were welling. Then they found him on the sand in his last resting-place, and bereft of soul, who had given them rings in days gone by, and then had the last day drawn to its close, for the good man Beowulf, the warrior King, the Lord of the Weder-Goths, had died a wondrous death.

But before this they had seen a more marvellous sight, the dragon on the sea-plain, the loathsome one lying right opposite. And there was the fire-dragon grimly terrible, and scorched with fire. And he was fifty feet in length as he lay there stretched out. He had had joy in the air awhile by night, but afterwards he went down to visit his den. But now he was the prisoner of death, and had enjoyed his last of earth-cares. And by him stood drinking-cups and flagons, and dishes were lying there and a costly sword, all rusty and eaten through as though they had rested a thousand winters in the bosom of the earth. And those heirlooms were fashioned so strongly, the gold of former races of men, and all wound round with spells, so that no man could come near that Ring-hall, unless God only, Himself the true King of victories, gave power to open up the hoard to whom He would (for He is the Protector of men) even to that man as it seemed good to Him.

42

Then was it quite clear to them that the affair had not prospered with the monster, who had hidden ornaments within the cave under the cliff. The guardian thereof had slain some few in former days. Then had the feud been wrathfully avenged. And it is a mystery anywhere when a valiant earl reaches the end of his destiny, when a man may no longer with his kinsmen dwell in the mead-hall. And thus was it with Beowulf when he sought out the guardian of the cavern and his cunning crafts. And he himself knew not how his departure from this world would come about. And thus famous chieftains uttered deep curses until the day of doom, because they had allowed it to come to pass that the monster should be guilty of such crimes, and, accursed and fast with hell-bands, as he was, and tormented with plagues that he should plunder the plain. He (Beowulf) was not greedy of gold, and had more readily in former days seen the favour of God.

Wiglaf spake, the son of Weohstan: 'Often shall many an earl of his own only will suffer misery, as is our fate. Nor could we teach the dear lord and shepherd of the kingdom any wisdom so that he would fail to be meeting the keeper of the gold treasures (the dragon) or to let him stay where he had been a long time dwelling in his cavern until the world's end. But he held to his high destiny. Now the hoard is seen by us, grimly got hold of, and at too great a cost was it yielded to the King of the people whom he enticed to that conflict. I was within the cavern, and looked upon all the hoard, the decoration of the palace, when by no means pleasantly, room was made for me, and a faring was granted to me in under the sea-cliff. And in much haste I took a very great burden of hoard-treasures in my hand, and bore it forth hither to my King. He was still alive, wise and witting well. And he the ancient uttered many words in sadness, and bade me greet you, and commanded that ye should build after death of your friend a high grave-mound in the place of the funeral pyre, a great and famous monument, for he himself was the most worshipful of men throughout the earth, while he was enjoying the wealth of his city. Let us now go and see and seek yet once again the heap of treasures, the wonder under the cliff. I will direct you, so that ye may look at close quarters upon the rings and the wealth of gold. Let the bier be quickly made ready when we come forth again, and then let us carry the dear man our lord when he shall enjoy the protection of the Ruler of all things.'

Then the son of Weohstan, the battle-dear warrior, ordered that commandment should be given to many a hero and householder that they should bring the wood for the funeral pyre from far, they the folk-leaders, to where the good man lay dead.

'Now the war-flame shall wax and the fire shall eat up the strong chief among warriors, him who often endured the iron shower, when the storm of arrows, strongly impelled, shot over the shield-wall, and the shaft did good service, and all eager with its feather, fear followed and aided the barb.' Then the proud son of Weohstan summoned from the troop the thanes of the King, seven of them together, and the very best of them, and he the eighth went under the hostile roof. And one of the warriors carried in his hand a torch which went on in front.

And no wise was it allotted who should plunder that hoard, since they saw some part unguarded remaining in the Hall, and lying there fleeting.

And little did any man mourn when full heartily they carried forth the costly treasures. Then they shoved the dragon the worm over the cliff-wall, and let the wave take him and the flood embrace that guardian of the treasures. Then the twisted golden ornaments were loaded on a wagon, an immense number of them. And the noble Atheling, the hoar battle-warrior, was carried to Whales' Ness.

43

Then the People of the Geats got ready the mighty funeral pyre, and hung it round with helmets and battle-shields, and bright byrnies as he had asked. And in the midst they lay the famous Prince, and they lamented the Hero, their dear lord. Then the warriors began to stir up the greatest of bale-fires on the cliff-side. And the reek of the wood-smoke went up swart, over the flame, which was resounding, and its roar mingled with weeping (and the tumult of winds was still), until it had broken the body, all hot into the heart. And unhappy in their thinkings, and with minds full of care, they proclaim the death of their lord, likewise a sorrowful song the Bride. . . .[82]

And heaven swallowed up the smoke. Then on the cliff-slopes the people of the Geats erected a mound, very high and very broad, that it might be beholden from afar by the wave-farers; and they set up the beacon of the mighty in battle in ten days. And the leavings of the funeral fire they surrounded with a wall, so that very proud men might find it to be most worthy of reverence.

And they did on the barrow rings and necklaces, and all such adornments as formerly warlike men had taken of the hoard. And they allowed the earth to hold the treasure of earls, the gold on the ground, where it still is to be found as useless to men as it always was.[83] Then the battle-dear men rode round about the mound, the children of the Athelings, twelve of them there were in all, and would be uttering their sorrows and lamenting their King, and reciting a dirge, and speaking of their champion. And they talked of his earlship and of his brave works, and deemed them doughty, as is fitting that a man should praise his lord in words and cherish him in his heart when he shall have gone forth from the fleeting body. So the People of the Geats lamented over the fall of their lord, his hearth-companions, and said that he was a world-king, and the mildest, the gentlest of men, and most tender to his people, and most eager for their praise.

End Notes

Introduction

1. See Arnold, p. 115.
2. See conclusion of *Tess of the D'Urbervilles*.

Prelude

1. See Appendix 2.
2. Not the hero of the poem.
3. Cp. with this the 'Passing of Arthur,' as related by Tennyson. The meaning is clear. Cp. also Appendix.

The Story

1. Not the hero of this poem.
2. The gables were decorated with horns of stags and other beasts of the chase.
3. See Appendix 5, and chapters 28, and 29.
4. Wyatt's translation of 'Ne his myne wisse.'
5. i.e. Beowulf.
6. Geats. The tribe to which Beowulf belonged. They inhabited southern Sweden between the Danes on the south and the Swedes on the north. See Appendix 11.
7. Literally, 'Then was the sea traversed at the end of the ocean.'
8. Frequent references are made to the device of the boar on shield and helmet; cp. p. 31, in description of Hnaef's funeral pyre.
9. The name of a reigning Danish dynasty.
10. For Scyld cp. Appendix 2.
11. Hygelac, King of the Geats at the time, and uncle of Beowulf.

12. Weland—'the famous smith of Germanic legend,' says Wyatt—who also refers us to the Franks Casket in the British Museum.

13. Weird was a peculiarly English conception. It means Fate, or Destiny. Then Weird became a god or goddess—cp. 'The Seafarer,' an Old English poem in which we find 'Weird is stronger, the Lord is mightier than any man's thoughts.'

14. i.e. Wealtheow, Hrothgar's Queen, who was of this tribe.

15. Healfdene was the father of Hrothgar, King of the Danes.

16. i.e. Beowulf.

17. Thus we see how sagas or legends came to be woven together into a song. See Appendix 10.

18. Heremod was a King of the Danes, and is introduced, says Wyatt, as a stock example of a bad King.

19. Wyatt's translation.

20. Byrny was a coat of mail. Swords were of greater value as they were ancient heirlooms, and had done good service.

21. See Appendix 6.

22. i.e. Hildeburh, wife of Finn.

23. i.e. Finn.

24. The boar then, as ever since, occupied a prominent place in heraldry.

25. See a similar passage in my version of *Sir Gawain and the Green Knight*, Canto II. 1 and 2.

26. Hrothulf, nephew of Hrothgar.

27. See Appendix 3.

28. See Appendix 4.

29. Wyatt's translation.

30. That is, 'the harp.'

31. Rune—literally, 'a secret.'

32. Cp. the phrase 'Welsh marches,' i.e. the boundaries or limits of Wales.

33. Cp. description of hunting in *Sir Gawain and the Green Knight*, Canto III. 2.

34. Scyldings are the Danes.

35. i.e. Unferth.

36. Cp. Chapter 8.

37. i.e. Hrothgar.

38. i.e. the sun.

39. Hrothgar.

40. Cp. pp. 23–25.

41. 'Honour-full' is Wyatt's translation.

42. Hrethric, one of Hrothgar's sons.

43. Literally, 'the gannet's bath.' The sea is also 'Swan's path,' 'Sail-path,' &c.

44. A difficult phrase. Refers perhaps to old feuds between Danes and Geats.

45. Cp. Chapter 3.

46. Thrytho is referred to as a foil to Hygd. Thrytho was as bad a woman as Hygd was good. She was a woman of a wild and passionate disposition. She became the Queen of King Offa, and it seems to have been a case of the 'taming of the shrew.' Offa appears to have been her second husband. See below.

47. i.e. to Offa.

48. i.e. Hygelac; see Appendicies 7 and 9.

49. i.e. Hygd, Queen of the Geats, Hygelac's wife.

50. i.e. Wealtheow, Hrothgar's Queen.

51. i.e. Ingeld. See below.

52. Another episode, viz. that of Freawaru and Ingeld. Note also the artificial break of the narrative into chapters. See Appendix 5. Hrothgar's hopes by the marriage of his daughter Freawaru to Ingeld of the Heathobards was doomed to disappointment, cp. 'Widsith,' 45-9.

53. Numbers 29 and 30 are lacking in the MS. The divisions here are as in Wyatt's edition.

54. Withergyld—name of a Heathobard warrior.

55. Probably referring to the chanting of some ancient legend by the scop, or gleeman.

56. Wyatt's translation.

57. Hygelac was killed in his historical invasion of the Netherlands, which is five times referred to in the poem. See Appendix 7.

58. See Appendix 9.

59. The MS. here is very imperfect. I have used the emended text of Bugge, which makes good sense. See Appendix 12.

60. Here again the text is imperfect.

61. Possibly a later insertion, 'the ten commandments' (Wyatt).

62. Beowulf saved his life by swimming across the sea, in Hygelac's famous raid. See Appendix 7.

63. See Appendix 9.

64. See Appendix 9.

65. See p. 60-61.

66. See Appendix 8.

67. See Appendix 7 and 9.

68. Waegmundings—the family to which both Beowulf and Wiglaf belonged.

69. See Appendix 9.

70. i.e. Beowulf.

71. Wyatt and Morris's translations.

72. Wyatt and Morris translate 'sun jewels.'

73. Wyatt's translation.

74. i.e. Wiglaf.

75. i.e. it had been well hammered into shape.

76. Yet another reference to Hygelac's famous raid. See Appendix 7.

77. Merovingian King of the Franks.

78. See Appendix 9.

79. Hrethel, King of Geats, father of Hygelac and grandfather of Beowulf.

80. Literally, 'the sword-leavings.'

81. See Appendix 9.

82. Text in MS. faulty here. Wyatt and Morris have adopted Bugge's emendation. The sense is that Beowulf's widow with her hair bound up utters forth a dirge over her dead husband.

83. Probably the treasures that remained in the cavern. See previous chapter.

APPENDIX

1

General Note on the Poem

This is the greatest poem that has come down to us from our Teutonic ancestors. Our only knowledge of it is through the unique MS in the British Museum.

It has already been translated at least eight times as follows:

1. Kemble, 1837.
2. Thorpe and Arnold (with the O.E. Poem accompanying it).
3. Lumsden, 1881 (in ballad form).
4. Garnett, 1883.
5. Earle, 1892.
6. William Morris and A. J. Wyatt, 1895. This is in poetic form, but abounds in archaisms and difficult inversions, and is sometimes not easy to read or indeed to understand.
7. Wentworth Huyshe, 1907.
8. A translation in 1912. Author unknown.

Many of the persons and events of *Beowulf* are also known to us through various Scandinavian and French works as follows:

Scandinavian Records

1. Saxo's *Danish History*.
2. Hrólf's *Saga Kraka*.
3. *Ynglinga Saga* (and *Ynglinga tál*).
4. *Skiöldunga Saga*.

As instances of identical persons and events:

1. Skiöldr, ancestor of Skiöldungar, corresponds to Scyld the ancestor of Scyldungas.
2. The Danish King Halfdan corresponds to Healfdene.
3. His sons Hroarr and Helgi correspond to Hrothgar and Halga.
4. Hrölf Kraki corresponds to Hrothwulf, nephew of Hrothgar.
5. Frothi corresponds to Froda, and his son Ingialdi to Ingeld.
6. Otarr corresponds to Ohthere, and his son Athils to Eadgils.

With the exception of the *Ynglinga tál* all these records are quite late, hence they do not afford any evidence for the dates of events mentioned in *Beowulf*.

Further Scandinavian correspondences are seen in Böthvarr Biarki, the chief of Hrölf Kraki's knights. He is supposed to correspond to Beowulf. He came to Leire, the Danish royal residence, and killed a demon in animal form. Saxo says it was a bear. This demon attacked the King's yard at Yule-tide, but Biarki and Beowulf differ as to their future, for Biarki stayed with Hrölf Kraki to the end and died with him.

In the *Grettis Saga* the hero kills two demons, male and female. It is true that the scene is laid in Iceland, but minor details of scenery, the character of the demons, and other similarities make it impossible to believe the two stories to be different in origin. They both sprang out of a folk-tale associated after ten centuries with Grettis, and in England and Denmark with a historical prince of the Geats.

French Records

1. *Historia Francorum* and *Gesta Regum Francorum* (discovered by Outzen and Leo).

   In A.D. 520 a raid was made on the territory of the Chatuarii. Their king Theodberht, son of Theodric I, defeated Chocilaicus, who was killed. This Chocilaicus is identified with the Hygelac of our poem, and the raid with Hygelac's raid on the Hetware (= Chatuarii), the Franks, and the Frisians. This helps us to estimate the date for *Beowulf* as having been born somewhere about the end of the fifth century.

2. *Historia Francorum*, by Gregory of Tours. The author speaks of the raider as the King of the Danes.

3. *Liber Monstrorum*. In this work the raider is Rex Getarum, King of the Geats, who may correspond with the Geats of our poem.

The Geats were the people of Gautland in Southern Sweden. See Appendix 11.

Origin of the Anglo-Saxon Poem

It was probably written in Northumbrian or Midland, but was preserved in a West Saxon translation.

There would seem to be some justifiable doubt as to the unity of the poem. Though on the whole pagan and primitive in tone, it has a considerable admixture of Christian elements, e.g. on pp. 3-4 and 5-6 and pp. 47-49, though the latter passage may be a late interpolation. Generally speaking, the poetry and sentiments are Christian in tone, but the customs are pagan. The author of the article in *The Cambridge History of English Literature*, vol. i., to whom I owe much, says: 'I cannot believe that any Christian poet could have composed the account of Beowulf's funeral.' One passage is very reminiscent of Eph. vi. 16, viz. Chapter 25. p. 48; whilst page 3-4 (lower half) may be compared with Cædmon's *Hymn*. There are also references to Cain and Abel and to the Deluge. Of Chapters 1-31 the percentage of Christian elements is four, whilst of the remaining Chapters (32 ad fin.) the percentage is ten, due chiefly to four long passages. Note especially that the words in Chapter 2, 'And sometimes they went vowing at their heathen shrines and offered sacrifices,' et seq., are quite inconsistent with the Christian sentiment attributed to Hrothgar later in the poem. 'It is generally thought,' says the writer in *The Cambridge History of English Literature*, 'that several originally separate lays have been combined into one poem, and, while there is no proof of this, it is quite possible and not unlikely.'

There are in the poem four distinct lays:

1. Beowulf's Fight with Grendel.
2. Beowulf's Fight with Grendel's mother.
3. Beowulf's Return to the land of the Geats.
4. Beowulf's Fight with the Dragon.

Competent critics say that probably 1 and 2 ought to be taken together, while Beowulf's reception by Hygelac (see 3 above) is probably a separate lay. Some scholars have gone much further in the work of disintegration, even attributing one half of the poem to interpolators, whilst others suggest two parallel versions. Summing up, the writer in *The Cambridge History of English Literature* says: 'I am disposed to think that a large portion of the poem existed in epic form before the change of faith, and that the appearance of Christian elements in the poem is due to revision. The Christianity of *Beowulf* is of a singularly indefinite and individual type, which contrasts somewhat strongly with what is found in later Old English poetry. This revision must have been made at a very early date.'

The poem was built up between A.D. 512, the date of the famous raid of Hygelac (Chocilaicus) against the Hetware (Chatuarii), and 752, when the French Merovingian dynasty fell; for, says Arnold, 'The poem contains not a word which by any human ingenuity could be tortured into a reference to any event subsequent to the fall of the Merovingians' (A.D. 752).

2

The Prelude

The Prelude would seem to be an attempt to link up the hero of the poem with the mythological progenitors of the Teutonic nations. Thomas Arnold says: 'That Sceaf, Scyld, and Beaw were among the legendary ancestors of the West Saxon line of kings no one disputes. But this does not mean much, for the poem itself shows that the same three were also among the legendary ancestors of the Danish kings.' Ethelward, who wrote early in the tenth century, gives the ancestry of Ethelwulf, the father of Alfred. Ethelward says: 'The seventeenth ancestor from Cerdic was Beo, the eighteenth Scyld, the nineteenth Scef.' Ethelward also says: 'Scef himself, with one light vessel, arrived in the island of the ocean which is called Scani, dressed in armour, and he was a very young boy, and the inhabitants of that land knew nothing about him; however, he was received by them, and kept with care and affection as though he were of their own kin, and afterwards they chose him to be king, from whose stock the King Athulf [Ethelwulf] derives his line.'

It may be noted that neither Scyld nor Scef is mentioned in the A.S. Chronicle (A.D. 855). William of Malmesbury, in his Gesta Regum, says that Scef was so called from the sheaf of wheat that lay at his head, that he was asleep when he arrived, and that when he grew up he became a king in the town then called Slaswic, now Haithebi (Rolls Ed., 1. 121).

Müllenhoff says: 'If we look closely into the saga, the ship and the sheaf clearly point to navigation and agriculture, the arms and jewels to kingly rule—all four gifts, therefore, to the main elements and foundations of the oldest state of culture among the Germans [Teutons?] of the sea-board; and if the bearer of these symbols became the first king of the country, the meaning can only be this, that from his appearance the beginning of the oldest state of culture dates, and that generally before him no orderly way of leading a human life had existed.'

Scyld (meaning Shield) refers to the fact that the king was the protector of the people in war, and is therefore symbolical, like Scef.

The ship and the sheaf, the arms and the jewels and the shield—these are the symbols of that primitive civilization—the sheaf, the symbol of agriculture and food, the ship of commerce, the arms of warfare, the jewels of reward of bravery, and the shield of the protection of the people by the king.

Arnold mentions the fact that no writer not English mentions the saga of Scef and Scyld, and suggests that this is presumption for the English origin of the legend. I do not, however, think it is conclusive evidence. One is surprised that they are not mentioned in Icelandic literature. Yet somehow the impression on my mind is that these legends were probably brought by our Saxon and Danish ancestors from the Continent, and are taken for granted as well known to the hearers of the song. I think they probably formed part of the legendary genealogy of our common Germanic (Teutonic) ancestors, and happened to find their way into literature only among the English, or have survived only in the English.

3

'Brosinga Mene'

'Brosinga Mene,' p. 34, is the 'Brisinga-mén' mentioned in the *Edda*, an Icelandic poem. 'This necklace is the Brisinga-mén—the costly necklace of Freja, which she won from the Dwarfs, and which was stolen from her by Loki, as is told in the *Edda*' (Kemble).

Loki was a Scandinavian demi-god. He was beautiful and cunning. He was the principle of strife, the spirit of evil; cp. Job's Satan. Freya was the Scandinavian Goddess of Love. She claimed half of the slain in battle. She was the dispenser of joy and happiness. The German *frau* is derived from Freya. Hama carried off this necklace when he fled from Eormanric. The origin of this legend, though worked up in the *Edda*, seems to have been German or Gothic, and 'Brosinga' has reference to the rock-plateau of Breisgau on the Rhine. It is probably a relic of the lost saga of Eormanric (see Appendix 4), the famous Ostrogothic king referred to in Chapter 28. Eormanric is one of the few historical personages of the poem.

4

Eormanric

Gibbon mentions Eormanric in his chapter 25. of the *Decline and Fall*, and, in spite of chronological discrepancies, this Eormanric is probably identical with the one mentioned in *Beowulf* (Chapter 18), in Jornandes (Chapter 24), and in the *Edda*.

In Jornandes the story is as follows.

Characters

1. ERMANARIC.
2. A Chief of the Roxolani tribe who was a traitor.
3. SANIELH (= SWANHILD) wife of the chief.
4. SARUS, brother of Sanielh.
5. AMMIUS, brother of Sanielh.

Ermanaric puts Sanielh to death by causing her to be torn to pieces by wild horses, because of the treachery of her husband, the chief of the Roxolani. Her brothers, Ammius and Sarus, avenge her death by attacking Ermanaric, but they only succeed in wounding him and disabling him for the rest of his life.

In the *Edda* the story is as follows.

Characters

1. GUDRUN, widow of Sigurd and Atli.
2. SWANHILD, daughter of Gudrun by Sigurd.
3. JONAKUR, Gudrun's third husband.
4. SÖRLI, son of Gudrun and Jonakur.
5. HAMTHIR, son of Gudrun and Jonakur.
6. ERP, son of Gudrun and Jonakur.

7. JORMUNREK (EORMANRIC).
8. RANDVER, son of Jormunrek.

Jormunrek hears of the beauty of Swanhild and sends his son Randver to seek her out for him in marriage. Gudrun consents; on the way Randver is incited by the traitor Bicci to betray Swanhild, and is then accused by him to the king. For this treachery Jormunrek hangs Randver and causes Swanhild to be trampled to death by wild horses. Then the three sons of Gudrun set out to avenge their sister. On the way his two brothers kill Erp, and are consequently unable to kill Jormunrek. They only succeed in maiming him.

Saxo Grammaticus, to whom we also owe the story of Hamlet, tells a similar story.

Characters

1. JARMERIC, a Danish King.
2. SWAWILDA (= SWANHILD), wife of Jarmeric.
3. HELLESPONTINE BROTHERS, brothers of Swawilda.
4. BICCO, a servant of Jarmeric.

Bicco accuses Swawilda to Jarmeric of unfaithfulness. He causes her to be torn to pieces by wild horses. Then her brothers kill Jarmeric with the help of a witch, Gudrun, hewing off his hands and feet.

These three stories are evidently based on one common original.

5

Marriage of Freawaru and Ingeld

Characters

1. FREAWARU, daughter of Hrothgar the Dane.
2. INGELD, son of Froda, King of the Heathobards.
3. FRODA, King of the Heathobards.
4. A Heathobard warrior.
5. Son of the Danish warrior who had killed Froda.

The Heathobards were a people in Zealand. There had been an ancient feud between the Danes and the Heathobards in which Froda had been killed by a Danish warrior. Hrothgar hoped to appease the feud by the marriage of his daughter Freawaru to Ingeld. Unluckily, the son of the Danish warrior who had killed Froda accompanied Freawaru to Ingeld's Court. Then an old Heathobard warrior notices this and stirs up strife. The marriage fails in its object, and war breaks out again between the Danes and the Heathobards. Beowulf predicts the course of events in his speech to Hygelac (Chapters 28 and 29).

6

Finn

The Finn episode (Chapters 16 and 17) is one of those events in *Beowulf* that would be quite well known to the first hearers of the song, but to us is lacking in that clearness we might desire. Fortunately, Dr. Hickes discovered a fragment entitled, 'The Fight at Finnsburgh,' on the back of a MS. of the *Homilies*. From *Beowulf* and from this fragment we are able to piece together an intelligible story. It is probably as follows:

Characters

1. FINN, King of the North Frisians and Jutes.
2. HOC, a Danish chieftain.
3. HILDEBURH, daughter of Hoc.
4. HNAEF, son of Hoc.
5. HENGEST, son of Hoc.
6. Two sons of Finn and Hildeburh.
7. HUNLAFING, a Finnish warrior.
8. GUTHLAF and OSLAF, two Danish warriors.

Finn abducts Hildeburh, the daughter of Hoc, the Dane. Hoc pursues the two fugitives and is killed in the mêlée. Twenty years pass by—Hnaef and Hengest, sons of Hoc, take up the 'vendetta.' In the fighting Hnaef and a son of Finn and Hildeburh are slain. A peace is patched up. Hengest, son of Hoc, is persuaded to remain as a guest of Finn for the winter, and it is agreed that no reference shall be made by either side to the feud between them. Then the bodies of Hnaef, Hildeburh's brother, and of her son are burnt together on the funeral pyre, 'and great is the mourning of Hildeburh for her son.' But Hengest is ever brooding vengeance. The strife breaks out anew in the spring.

Hengest is killed, but two of his warriors, Guthlaf and Oslaf, break through the enemy, return to Finn's country, and slay him and carry off Hildeburh. 'The Fight at Finnsburgh,' which is Homeric in style, is the account of the first invasion of Finn by Hnaef and Hengest, and Wyatt fits it in before the Finn episode on p. 30. Möller places it after the phrase, 'whose edge was well known to the Jutes,' on p. 32.

7

Hygelac

Hygelac, son of Hrethel, was king of the Geats, and uncle of Beowulf, his sister's son. He was the reigning king of Beowulf's fellow countrymen the Geats during the greater part of the action of the poem. Beowulf is often called 'Hygelac's kinsman,' and when he went forth to his battle with Grendel's mother (Chapter 22.), he bade Hrothgar in case of his death send the treasures he had given to him to Hygelac. Hygelac married Hygd, who is presented to us as a good Queen, the daughter of Hæreth. She was 'very young,' 'of noble character,' and 'wise.' She is compared, to her advantage, with Thrytho, who was a shrewish woman. No one dared to look upon her except her husband. However, her second husband, Offa, seems to have 'tamed the shrew' (see p. 103). Hygelac has been identified with Chocilaicus, who was killed in the famous raid on the Chatuarii referred to in the *Historia Francorum* and the *Gesta Regum*, who are identified with the Hetware of this poem (see p. 63 and Appendix 1.).

The famous raid of Hygelac upon the Hetware in which he met his death is referred to five times in the poem, as follows: Chapters 18, p. 34; 31, p. 59; 33, p. 63; 35, p. 66; 40, p. 77.

On the death of Hygelac his son Heardred succeeded to the throne (Chapter 31, p. 59); and, after a brief interval, he was killed in battle by Onela (see Appendix 9). Then Beowulf succeeded to the throne of the Geats (Chapter 31, p. 59). Hygelac died between a.d. 512 and 520. Beowulf died about 568. He reigned fifty years.

8

Hæthcyn and Herebald

It would seem doubtful as to whether this was deliberate or accidental. The poet says 'Hæthcyn missed the mark' with his javelin and killed his brother Herebald; but subsequently he speaks as though it had been deliberate murder.

9

Wars Between the Swedes and the Geats

Characters

Swedes

1. ONGENTHEOW, King of the Swedes.
2. ONTHERE, his son.
3. ONELA, his son.
4. EADGILS, son of Onthere.
5. EANMUND, son of Onthere.

Geats, &c.

6. HÆTHCYN, King of Geats.
7. HYGELAC, King of Geats.
8. HEARDRED, King of Geats.
9. BEOWULF, King of Geats.
10. EOFOR, Geat warrior.
11. WULF, Geat warrior.

Ongentheow was a King of the Swedes. The Swedes are also called Scylfings in the poem. The origin of the word 'Scylfing' is doubtful. Ongentheow went to war with Hæthcyn, King of the Geats and brother of Hygelac; and Ongentheow, who was well advanced in years, struck down his foe (Chapter 40, p. 77) at the battle of Ravenswood. This was the first time that the Swedes invaded the Geats. The Geats retreated into the Ravenswood at nightfall, but with the dawn they heard the horn of Hygelac 'as the good prince came marching on the track.' Ongentheow now was alarmed, for Hygelac's prowess in battle was far-famed. He withdrew into some fortification, and was attacked by the

Geats. Two brothers, Eofor and Wulf, assailed the veteran warrior. He defended himself with great vigour and killed Wulf; but Eofor came to the help of his brother and dealt Ongentheow his death-blow over the guard of his shield.

Ongentheow's two sons were Onela and Ohthere. Ohthere had two sons, Eanmund and Eadgils.

These two sons of Ohthere were banished from Sweden for rebellion, and took refuge at the Court of the Geat King Heardred. This greatly enraged their uncle Onela, that they should resort to the Court of their hereditary foes (see above). Onela invaded the land of the Geats (Chapters 33. and 34, pp. 63 sq.) and slew Heardred. Then it was that Beowulf became King of the Geats. Thus two Geatish kings had been slain by the Swedes, viz. Hæthcyn and Heardred. In revenge, later on, Beowulf supported Eadgils in his counter-attack on his own fatherland when Eadgils killed his uncle Onela. This story is confirmed by the Scandinavian accounts in which Athils (= Eadgils) slew Ali (= Onela) on the ice of Lake Wener; cp. the phrase 'cold journeyings' (Chapter 34, p. 64).

This is Wyatt's version of the story.

10

Sigmund

Sigmund (page 24) is the father and uncle of Fitela. He is stated in *Beowulf* to have killed a serpent who kept guard over a hoard of treasure. In the Icelandic saga known as the *Völsunga Saga*, Sigmund is represented as the father of Sigurd, and 'it is Sigurd who rifles the treasure of the Niblungs and kills the serpent (Fafnir), its guardian' (Arnold, p. 69), and he carries it away on the back of his horse Grani. Sigmund is represented as the son of a Völsung; that is, as *Beowulf* has it, 'the heir of Waels.' Waels was afterwards forgotten, however, and Waelsing was regarded as a proper name instead of a patronymic denoting descent from Waels. In a similar way, as Arnold points out, Sigmund is pushed into the background to make room for his son Sigurd (Siegfried). 'And so in the German *Nibelungen Lay* it is Sigurd (Siegfried) who wins the hoard, but does so by defeating and killing its former possessors Schilbung and Nibelung' (Arnold, p. 70). Attempts have been made to claim a German origin for this saga, but in face of the evidence of *Beowulf* and the *Völsunga Saga* and the *Edda* there is, I think with Arnold, little doubt but that its origin was Scandinavian. Possibly and probably we owe the later elaboration of the saga in the *Nibelungen Lay* to German influence. For discussion of the whole question see Arnold's *Notes on Beowulf*, pp. 67-75, Edit. 1898, cap. v.

11

Tribes Mentioned in the Poem

1. *Brondings.* Breca was a Bronding. After his famous swimming-match with Beowulf (Chapter 8), he is said to have sought out his 'pleasant fatherland the land of the Brondings.' Arnold suggests that they were located in Mecklenburg or Pomerania.
2. *Danes*, also called Bright-Danes, Ring-Danes, Spear-Danes, because of their warlike character; and North Danes, South Danes, &c., because of their wide distribution. They are said to have inhabited the Scede lands and Scedenig and 'between the seas'; that is, they were spread over the Danish Islands, the southern province of Sweden, and the seas between them.
3. *Jutes* (Eotenas), probably people ruled over by Finn, King of Friesland, and identical with the Frisians.
4. *Franks* and Frisians. The Franks were ancestors of the modern French. After the conversion of Clovis (A.D. 496), they gradually encroached on the Frisians.
5. *Frisians* include the Frisians, the Franks, the Hetware, and the Hugs. Friesland was the country between the River Ems and the Zuyder Zee.
6. *Geats.* They dwelt in the south of Sweden between the Danes and the Swedes. Bugge sought to identify them with the Jutes, and held that Gautland was Juteland. He based this theory on certain phrases: e.g. Chapter 32, where the Swedes (the sons of Ohthere) are said to have visited the Geats 'across the sea,' and again in Chapter 35 the Swedes and the Geats are said to have fought 'over wide water'; but, as Arnold points out, these phrases can be interpreted in such a way as not to be incompatible with the theory that they dwelt on the same side of the Cattegat, i.e. on the northern side, and in the extreme south of Sweden.

The question as to whether they are identical with the Goths of Roman history is still an open one. Arnold says, 'There is a great weight of evidence tending to identify the Geats with the Goths,' and he quotes evidence from Gibbon (chapter 10). Pytheas of Marseilles, in the fourth century, says that, passing through the Baltic Sea, he met with tribes of Goths, Teutons, and Ests.

Tacitus, in chapter 43 of *Germania*, speaks of the Goths as dwelling near the Swedes. Jornandes traces the Goths to Scanzia, an island in the Northern Sea. It is probable, then, that the Goths had a northern and indeed a Scandinavian origin. If so, Beowulf the Geat was probably a Goth.

7. *Healfdenes.* The tribe to which Hnaef belonged.
8. *Heathoremes.* The people on whose shores Beowulf was cast up after his swimming-match with Breca.
9. *Ingwine.* Friends of Ing—another name for the Danes.
10. *Scyldingas.* Another name for the Danes, as descended from Scyld.
11. *Scylfingas.* Name for the Swedes.
12. *Waegmundings.* The tribe to which both Beowulf and Wiglaf belonged.
13. *Wylfings.* Probably a Gothic tribe.

12

Page 59–60

The text here is much mutilated, and can only be restored by ingenious conjecture. Grein and Bugge and others have reconstructed it. On the whole Bugge's text, which I have followed, seems to me the most reasonable. It is unfortunate that the text should be so imperfect just at this critical point in the linking up of the two great divisions of the story. In the ancient days some remote predecessors of the Geats seem to have heaped up in the neighbourhood a pile of wonderful vessels jewel-bedecked, and treasures of all kinds, of inconceivable value. Then the last of the race carries the treasure to a barrow or cavern in the cliffs near the site, in after-generations, of Beowulf's palace, and delivers a pathetic farewell address (pp. 60 et seq.). The dragon finds the cavern and the treasure and appropriates it for three hundred years. Then one of Beowulf's retainers finds the treasure and takes a golden goblet while the dragon is sleeping, and offers it to his lord as a peace-offering. This brought about Beowulf's feud with the dragon in which he met his death.

Books Consulted

Beowulf, edited with textual footnotes, &c., by A. J. Wyatt, M.A. (Cantab. and London). Pitt Press, Cambridge, 1898.

The Tale of Beowulf, sometime King of the Folk of the Weder-Geats. Translated by William Morris, A. J. Wyatt. 1898. Longmans.

Zupitza's Transliteration of Beowulf. A photographic reproduction of the manuscript. Early English Text Society.

Encyclopaedia Britannica.

Chambers's Encyclopaedia.

Beowulf, Notes on, by Thomas Arnold, M.A., 1898. Longmans, Green & Co. This contains a good map of the scenes alluded to in the poem.

History of Early English Literature, by the Rev. Stopford Brooke.

Epic and Romance, W. P. Ker.

Ten Brink's *English Literature.*

Also available from Clydesdale Classics